# a TEMPORARY marriage

SUMMER DOWELL

Printed in the United States of America

First Printing, 2020
ISBN: 9781697369335

To my children.
Who keep me humble by reminding me
that my books would be better if there
were pictures.

# Table of Contents


**Chapter 1** 8

**Chapter 2** 21

**Chapter 3** 34

**Chapter 4** 49

**Chapter 5** 81

**Chapter 6** 100

**Chapter 7** 110

**Chapter 8** 143

**Chapter 9** 156

**Chapter 10** 172

**Chapter 11** 188

**Chapter 12** 199

**Chapter 13** 216

**Chapter 14** 232

**Chapter 15** 249

**Chapter 16** 263

Epilogue 277

# Chapter 1

Kylee Morgan sat in her usual seat at the local coffee shop, her laptop propped open in front of her. She'd been there all morning, the wrapper of her blueberry muffin and now lukewarm hot chocolate proof of that. The logo she'd been painstakingly working on filled her screen. This new client could be a huge boost for her income, which was why it needed to be perfect.

Suddenly, her phone buzzed in her purse. She slipped it out, lighting up the screen with the press of her thumb. Across it, flashed a new text message:

***Hey, you want to meet for lunch today? I have a non-work-related favor to ask*.**

She stared down at the text, a burst of pleasure seeping through her at the words. Ryan wanted to have lunch with her?

Not that it should have been a big deal. Kylee had done several design projects for him over the years, and they often met for lunch here and there. Their work relationship had evolved into a real friendship. Strictly friendship, of course. There was no way Kylee was harboring any romantic feelings for her extremely attractive *friend*. Definitely not.

She read the text once more. *What kind of favor would he need from me?* she thought as a reply flew from under her fingers.

***Sure, when and where?***

***Let's go to Rodrigo's. Can you be there by noon?***

She glanced at the time. That was in twenty minutes, but she should be able to make it. It wasn't like she had anything pressing on her schedule at the moment. Freelancing did have a few bonuses.

***Sounds good. See you then.***

As she put the phone down, she glanced at what she was wearing. Dismay hit her at the outfit she had thrown on that morning. Her comfortable old jeans, long since faded and worn, did absolutely nothing for her figure. And the oversized, purple sweatshirt just made things worse. Her plan had been to spend the bulk of the day holed up in a coffee shop, editing photos.

Kylee sighed. There was no way she'd have enough time to go home, change, and get over to Rodrigo's.

Not that it mattered. Ryan thought of her as nothing other than a good friend who did some graphic design work for him on the side. He probably wouldn't blink twice if she showed up in her pajamas.

She stood, shoving the laptop into her bag. Tossing the cold cup of hot chocolate into the trash, Kylee strode out of the shop, doing her best to ignore her frumpy reflection in the glass door.

*****

Ryan sat in his chair, tapping his fingers mindlessly on the vinyl tabletop in front of him. He'd gotten to Rodrigo's a few minutes early, so he'd gone ahead and ordered burritos for the both of them. Extra cheese for him, no beans and extra guacamole for Kylee.

His phone buzzed with a text. When he pulled it out, he saw it was from his brother.

***Did she agree to it?? Is she as nuts as you?***

Ryan blew a breath of air out as he responded.

***No, she's not here yet. Stop bugging me.***

He turned off his phone before sliding it back into his pocket.

A blonde girl entered the place, and for a second, he thought it was her. But when she turned, there was no hint of Kylee's grin or bright-green eyes. He ran a hand through his hair and leaned back into the chair. He needed to relax; his nerves were pushing him to the edge.

Ryan had a good reason to be nervous, though. He was pretty sure there was at least a 70% chance Kylee would turn his request down. If he hadn't been so desperate, there was no way he would've considered asking her in the first place. Really, who in their right mind asked one of their best friends to—

"Hey, Ryan." Kylee rapped her knuckles on the tabletop, pulling Ryan out of his musings.

"Kylee, oh, good. You came!" He jumped up and reached for an impromptu hug.

She gave him a funny look, and he shrugged, trying to play it off. He and Kylee were good friends, but they weren't normally the touchy-feely type.

"Well, I said I'd come." She shrugged as she settled into the chair across from him. "So here I am."

"Yeah, of course. I just...never mind." Despite the fact that Ryan wanted to dive right into his request, he knew they'd need a little small talk first. Something to ease into his plea. "I ordered us both burritos, so I hope you haven't discovered a love for beans in the last couple of weeks."

"Definitely not." She wrinkled her nose. "If I ever do develop an affinity for them, please have my taste buds checked."

Her easy smile put him a little more at ease. This was Kylee. She was one of his best friends. Everything would be fine.

"Did you catch any of the Nuggets' game last night?" He and Kylee both shared a strong affinity for basketball. Specifically, their local team, the Denver Nuggets. Kylee wasn't as hardcore a fan as him, but he knew she liked to keep an eye on their season.

"I didn't, but I heard the last five minutes were insane." She leaned forward, resting her elbows on the table. "From what I heard, the refs totally threw the game for us."

He shrugged, momentarily forgetting his worries. "I don't know if I'd go that far, but they sure made a few questionable calls. It didn't help that our defense basically stopped playing in the fourth quarter."

Kylee shook her head. "I need a new team."

Ryan grinned and threw a sugar packet at her. "Don't you dare go betraying your roots!"

She laughed and sailed it back at him.

"So, how's work going? Any new clients lately?" he asked.

"I got a project for a children's boutique I'm excited about, and I'm still finishing up that dental office's website." She fiddled with a napkin as she talked. "Nothing too crazy, but enough to pay the bills—well, most of them."

Kylee's pause and furrowed brow made him assume she was still tight for money. She always insisted she loved her work, but he knew she had a load of school debt still weighing on her. Things were tight at best with her. Ryan wondered if he should jump in with his request.

She continued, though, and the moment was lost.

"But I can't complain. My client load is steadily increasing, which is exactly what I've hoped for. Anyway, what about you? How's Hudson's Packs going?"

"Oh...good. Our order for Outdoor Unlimited is still on. They've guaranteed to place us in one hundred of their stores across the U.S. I've also got a deal hinging with two other sporting goods stores. If I can prove myself with Outdoor Unlimited, their orders are a shoo-in."

"So, basically, everything depends on success with this initial order?" Kylee asked.

Ryan nodded, his stomach sinking again. "Yep. Everything." This was his opening. "Which is actually why I wanted to meet with you today. I have a favor to—"

"Two carnitas burritos with a side of chips and salsa?" A young waitress interrupted him mid-sentence, snapping her gum as she talked. She held a tray with two burritos and a plate of chips still glistening from the fryer.

"Uh, yeah, that's us." Ryan tried to paste a smile on his face. Obviously, the girl didn't realize she was interrupting an extremely uncomfortable conversation. Well, at least on his part. Kylee seemed perfectly fine as she shoved aside the salt and pepper shakers to make room on the table.

"Great," the girl called over her shoulder as she strolled off.

Rodrigo's wasn't exactly known for the best customer service. Luckily, the burritos made up for it.

Kylee peeked inside the burrito nearest her. "I'm assuming you got the one with extra sour cream?" She lifted one eyebrow as she slid it over to him.

"Of course. Who wouldn't want more of that goodness?"

Kylee didn't seem to be listening to his response. "Oh my gosh, this smells so good," she moaned as she unwrapped one edge of hers. She brought the burrito to her nose and inhaled dramatically.

Ryan couldn't help but smile. Kylee was pretty funny once you got to know her. You just had to get past her shy exterior. He mentally shook his head. No, it wasn't that she was shy. Kylee was just more of a listener. She was the type who would stand back in large groups and watch everyone else instead of vying for attention. Ryan studied her as she took a bite. It'd probably taken about a year of working with her until he'd gotten to know the more silly side of her.

"Mmm, how do they do this?" She waved her hands about. "I mean, like, the combination of that buttery, almost earthy guacamole, combined with that tangy pork—"

"I feel like you just met me for the food," Ryan said, biting back a grin.

"—and then there's the tang from the sauce, and that hint of spice from the peppers..."

He huffed. "Now, I'm getting a complex..."

"And don't even get me started on these homemade tortillas. Like seriously, wow!"

Ryan laughed out loud at this point and reached for a chip. "Well, I love spending time with you too, Kylee."

She grinned back at him, her green eyes sparkling. "Okay, enough food raving. What was it you were about to ask me? Before the waitress cut you off?"

Ryan's nerves came flooding back. He set his burrito on the tray and wiped his suddenly sweaty hands on his jeans. "Yeah, about that." He gulped. "So, I asked you to meet me today because I have a question for you. More of a request, actually. And I need to preface this," he said, lifting up his hands. "This is going to sound crazy. I am well aware of that. And if I had any other choice, there's no way I'd ask this favor of you."

Kylee's eyes had widened. She put her burrito down and placed her elbows on the table. "What is it, Ryan? You know you can ask me anything."

Ryan tried to grin, but it probably looked more like a grimace. "Kylee, will you marry me?"

*****

Kylee was pretty sure her heart had stopped. If she hadn't still been breathing, she would've checked for her pulse. "M-marry you?"

She must have heard him wrong. Ryan Hudson. Dreamy, beautiful Ryan Hudson. The man she'd had a strictly platonic friendship with the last three years. Strictly platonic. The man she was totally not denying any romantic feelings for. That man was asking her to marry him?

"Not for real, of course!"

His quick response popped her balloon of giddiness.

"What do you mean 'not for real'?" This had to have been the most bizarre two minutes they'd ever spent together.

He took a deep breath. "Okay, let me explain. Hudson Packs is currently in a bit of a...financial crisis." A flush crept up his neck. "The bag order we're doing for Outdoors Unlimited was supposed to be fulfilled this week. But when I went to the warehouse to do some quality control checking, there was a big mistake. The material used was not the dyneema composite fabric I thought I had ordered."

"The what?"

"It's a super lightweight, yet amazingly durable, fabric made from these non-woven composites…."

Kylee tried to listen, but her mind was whirling with how this had anything to do with getting married.

Ryan cut himself off mid-sentence. "Er, nevermind. You don't need to know all this. Basically, instead of my bags being made with a top-of-the-line backpacking material, every single one was made with some cheap nylon instead."

Blinking, she furrowed her brow. "Was it the manufacturer's fault? They should have to pay to fix them, right?"

Ryan placed a hand over his eyes. She could almost feel the waves of regret radiating off of him. "That's the issue. It wasn't the manufacturer's error. It was mine. Somehow, I listed out the wrong fabric to use, and now, I have two thousand units of cheaply made backpacks." He slid his hand down to his chin, gloom clouding his gaze over.

"Dang." That was all she could say.

Ryan nodded at her response. "Exactly. When I told Outdoors Unlimited about the issue, they said they would give me two months to redo the order. The problem is, I don't have the funds to manufacture a whole other two thousand units. And thanks to my last entrepreneurial fail"—Ryan's face was turning red now—"the company's credit isn't good enough to get a loan from the bank."

"Double dang." Kylee was back to leaning on her elbows, engrossed in Ryan's story and feeling for her friend. "So, what are you going to do?"

"Well, that's where you come in." He looked her in the eye. "My grandparents set up a trust fund for each grandkid just before my grandpa died. In it, they left us all a substantial amount of money—definitely enough to get this order up and going."

"Sounds like your grandparents were pretty well off."

"I like to think I got my entrepreneurial spirit from him. He started up a line of car wash locations when he was younger. He eventually sold the company for a ridiculously high sum. Apparently, he ended up investing the funds well."

"So, you have a trust fund with hordes of money to pay for this second order, and yet you're coming to your starving-artist friend, asking her to marry you because..."

Kylee stared at him with narrow eyes, not seeing where she fit.

"The trust has one catch." He shoved his burrito around the tray. "The money is to be given to us on our wedding day as a wedding gift."

Kylee's eyes widened in understanding. "You've got to be kidding."

"Nope. Let's just say my grandparents were somewhat hopeless romantics."

"But your grandma is still alive, right?" she asked. Her gaze fluttered away from his dark, penetrating eyes to her worn tennis shoes. "Can't you just explain the situation to her, and she can release that condition?"

Ryan shook his head. "No, I've looked into it. Unfortunately, the trust was created under my grandfather's name. He made it so no changes or adjustments could be made after he died."

"So…" she started before taking a deep breath, "you want to pretend to marry me for a day so you can get the money?"

"Well," Ryan said, cringing, "it's a little more complicated than that. The money can't be transferred unless there are actual, legitimate documents confirming our marriage. As a matter of fact, I think, for legal purposes, we have to be married for at least a month." One corner of his mouth crept upward. "I think that was to discourage any gold diggers or fake-marriage schemes."

The irony was not missed on Kylee.

He rushed on to finish. "So, when I said that it wasn't for real, I meant we would actually have to get married. It would just be fake to us. Like, a marriage in name only. I wouldn't expect—you know—anything of you."

Now it was Kylee's turn to blush. She tried to cover it up by asking, "So what happens after a month? We just get divorced?"

Ryan shrugged. "I figured we could get an annulment. I believe that's easier than a divorce." He reached forward, almost as if he was going to grab her hand then thought better of it. "Look, Kylee, I know what I'm asking is crazy. And I don't want to abuse your friendship. So, in return, I'm offering to take care of your school debt."

She'd been busy speculating if he'd really been about to grab her hand or not, but she sat up straight at his last comment. "You'll what?"

"I'll take care of your student loans for you after this. The funds in the trust are plenty to cover your debt. I know they've been a huge deal for you the last few years."

Ryan had hit her sore spot. Student loans had been hanging over her head like a dark cloud. Graphic design was something she loved and was thrilled every day to be doing, but it didn't pay the best. And since she was constantly dropping money into the endless pit of student loans, she felt like she'd never get ahead in life.

He seemed to be studying her. "What are you thinking?" he finally asked.

She bit her lip as she looked up at him. "I-I don't know. I want to help you, Ryan...but this is a big, *big* favor. I don't know if I can do it." She stood, suddenly, no longer able to think with him staring at her. One part of her was screaming to say yes. Of course she wanted to marry Ryan Hudson, the man she'd secretly been crushing on for the last three years. The other part of her was demanding that she say no. Nothing good could come of this. She'd only allow him to dig deeper into her heart before ripping it open with that annulment.

"I'm going to need some time to consider it. I'll call you later, but I'm not sure."

Ryan's expression made her cringe. He clearly assumed her answer was already no. Hoping to lighten the mood, she gave him a half smile and swiped her burrito off the tray. "I'm taking this with me, though."

Ryan gave her an equally half-hearted grin as she turned to leave.

Kylee's mind was racing as she walked through the glass doors. She needed the money. It would almost be life changing. But how could she do it without exposing her feelings and getting hurt along the way?

# Chapter 2

"It's nuts," Kylee announced. "We both know it's nuts. I don't even know why I'm considering it." She was lying in the middle of her living room floor, the pillow over her head muffling her voice.

"You're considering it because the man is offering you about forty thousand dollars," said her roommate, Elena.

Kylee wished she could say that part didn't matter to her. But it did. Graphic design was her passion, but it probably hadn't been the most financially sound career choice. Even with a part-time job at the library and becoming an expert on how to live a frugal life, she'd already calculated the exact date she'd pay off her student loans, and that was the twenty-first of never.

She peeked out from under her pillow as Elena continued on.

"Plus, he's hot. I wouldn't mind being married to something like that for a few months." She finished her opinion with a definitive bite of the Oreo in her hand.

"We wouldn't be married for real, Elena. It's not like he has any romantic angle to this. This is purely a business transaction." She took the pillow off her head and sat up. "Let's think about this rationally. We need to make a pro-con list."

Leaning over, Kylee grabbed the decorative chalkboard they had propped on the coffee table. She vigorously erased the writing that said *Welcome Home*.

"Hey! Do you know how long it took me to get that writing to look good?" Elena exclaimed, waving her half-eaten cookie.

"Think of it as an opportunity for more practice," Kylee said as she made a T-shaped column. On the left, she wrote *PROS* and then *CONS* on the right. "All right, what are the pros of me doing this? Obviously, it would be financially beneficial." She scribbled "*money*" underneath PROS. "What else?"

"He's *muy caliente*," Elena responded, waggling her eyebrows.

"It would be something a good friend would do," Kylee went on, ignoring Elena's comment. She brought the chalk to her chin, thinking. "I mean, he's clearly desperate." She was quiet for a moment.

"All right. Let's move on to the cons," Elena said, interrupting the silence. She brushed her dark hair out of her face. "First off, this is obviously an insane idea."

Kylee just rolled her eyes. "Okay, the cons. There would be a moral issue since we would, basically, be lying to his family." She scribbled on the board, not noticing the hint of chalk smudged under her chin. "Then there's the moral issue of me marrying a man I don't technically plan to be *married* to. Marriage is supposed to be forever, right? Not some free month trial." Not that she was a saint, but she'd always hoped marriage would be a lasting step for her. "Plus, I'm not sure what the living arrangements would be. I obviously can't live with him."

"But you'll be married to him."

"Yeah, but not *married* married."

"I'm not sure if there's a difference," Elena added dryly. "You're either married or you're not. There are no varying degrees of marriage. This isn't the Olympics where you can get bronze, silver, or gold."

Kylee folded her arms. "Well, clearly this is going to be an issue for me, then." She bit her lip as she thought. "Another con is what this might do to our friendship. What if Ryan and I end up hating each other's guts after this? I'd hate to lose him—as a friend, of course."

Elena narrowed her eyes. "Of course."

"Well, clearly the vote has been taken. This is a ridiculous idea that I cannot go through with." She laid the chalkboard down with a thud. "I'd better go text Ryan and tell him I can't do it."

"Are we going to talk about the real issue here, or just keep dancing around it?" Elena asked as Kylee stood.

"What do you mean?"

"I mean, come on, *mi amiga.* Are we going to talk about the fact that you have a major crush on Ryan and have since you first met him? I'm about ninety-nine percent sure the real reason you don't want to do this is because you're scared of what could happen between you two."

An overwhelming feeling of denial rose in Kylee, one she knew stemmed from the fact that Elena's comment had just hit the bullseye. "I don't know what you're talking about," she said, her nose in the air.

"I think you do. And I think you're afraid that either things are going to totally bomb between you two, or…"—she held up a finger—"things are going to go really good, and this pretend marriage may lead to something real."

Kylee stared at her roommate, biting her cheek. It almost pained her how clearly Elena had hit the mark.

"Kylee," Elena said, her voice soft now. "I'm your best friend, and I'd hate to see you get hurt. You need to really think about what you're doing here. Is this something you want to risk? Do you want to chance getting your heart broken for *real* by Ryan when things are done in a month?" She tilted her head. "Or on the flipside, do you want to chance seeing if something real *could* happen between you two?"

"I don't know." Kylee covered her face with her hands. "How can I possibly agree to this? What if I totally regret it?"

She heard the rattling of plastic and looked up to see Elena holding a cookie out to her. "We'll use my foolproof decision-making tool. If you get the cream side, you do it."

Kylee grabbed the opposite side of the sandwich cookie and twisted slowly. As she pulled away, the entire layer of cream came with her.

Elena gave her a wide smile. "Congratulations on your engagement."

*****

Ryan was in front of the computer at his kitchen table. A half-eaten container of fried rice and orange chicken sat next to him in a styrofoam container. His eyes were scanning the screen, but his thoughts were a million miles away.

What was Kylee thinking? Was she going to accept his offer? Should he have been so blunt? What would he do if she didn't agree?

He shook his head and tried to focus on the page. It was a government website about the documents needed to obtain a marriage license.

After a few more minutes of researching, his phone buzzed on the table. He quickly flipped it over and saw *Kylee* flashing on his screen.

"Hello?" he said as he turned the phone to speaker mode. He hoped she couldn't hear the shakiness in his voice.

"I'll do it," came the quick reply.

"You will?" he exclaimed a little too loudly. He was glad she couldn't see him pumping his fist in victory. He cleared his throat and tried again. "I mean, that's awesome. I'm very happy—"

"We need to lay some ground rules first," Kylee cut back in.

"O-okay, yeah. Ground rules. I'm good with that." He had moved on from fist pumping to shadow boxing. "What are you thinking?"

"First...do you... What are your plans for our living arrangement? More specifically...our sleeping arrangements."

He was just about to perform the knockout blow to his imaginary opponent when she asked him this. He lowered his hands. "Uh, well, I honestly hadn't considered that part. I mean, realistically, you could just stay at your place." Even as he was saying this, an image of his mom stopping by on one of her random visits flashed through his mind. His parents didn't live close, over an hour away. However, whenever his mom came into town for shopping, she liked to drop in on him and say hi—usually unannounced.

"Or wait." He ran a hand through his hair. "It might be better if you stayed at my place. Just to keep up appearances and all that. It'll be fine, though," he rushed on, imagining her look of dread. "My place is a two-bedroom."

He'd definitely have to clean out his office first. He used it more as a storage unit than an actual work station lately.

"Okay." She still sounded hesitant. "I think we should agree ahead of time that no bed sharing is required. Ever. I want separate sleeping quarters at all times."

"Done," he responded quickly. He didn't want her thinking he was planning to make a move on her while she was helping him out. "Is there anything else?"

"I think we have to have a hard deadline for when the marriage ends. I want this to be a sure thing."

"Yes, we can do that. Let's say exactly one month from our marriage date, we will get an annulment." He should have been writing this stuff down. He flipped over a napkin from his takeout order and began scribbling on it.

"And I think I should get my payment—for my school debt—once the annulment is finalized. Just to make sure everything is very transparent from the beginning."

Man, she really had thought this through. He was impressed—and grateful. This had been his idea, but just like usual, she was coming through for him.

"Perfect. I agree completely." When she added nothing else to her list, he continued. "Kylee, I just want to thank you for doing this for me. I know it's probably totally out of your comfort zone, but I appreciate your help all the same."

There was an indiscernible voice on the other end.

"What was that?" Ryan asked.

"Nothing! Just Elena asking me if I want some...some water. She's pouring water for herself and wants to know if I'm thirsty. That's all." Kylee sounded like she was talking through clenched teeth.

He swore he heard the word *hottie* murmured on the other end, but Kylee cut in quickly.

"Anyway, glad we got this figured out. Should we set a date?"

"Um, I have to figure a few more things out," he said, his mind racing to the government civil services website he had opened on another tab, "but should we say Friday?" It was Wednesday, so that would give them two days to wrap up any loose ends.

"Great...I'm getting married on Friday... *We're* getting married on Friday." Kylee's tone was one of disbelief.

"I'll call you tomorrow with more details, but I'll probably just see you on Friday." He paused, a sly smile creeping up his face. "I will be counting down the days until our matrimony, my dear buttercup."

"Bye, you dork."

Ryan could hear her laughing as she hung up. He was glad he'd managed to lighten her mood a little.

Now, he just needed to plan a wedding in the next 24 hours.

*****

Kylee woke up the following morning, wondering if it had all been a dream. Had Ryan really asked her to marry him yesterday? Had she really agreed?

She rolled over to check the time on her phone, those thoughts still bouncing around in her head, and saw she had a new text.

***Hey, do you have a copy of your birth certificate? We'll need it for the marriage license.***

Well, it wasn't a dream.

Yep. It was all happening.

But it was *fake*. To help him get his money and to pay off her crushing student loans.

She had to remember that. And she couldn't let her real feelings get in the way.

She shot off a reply saying yes then set her phone back down. With a groan, she flopped back onto her bed. Maybe she could smother her nerves with blankets.

After a second, she shot back up. No. She didn't have time to be lazy. She had too much to do. She needed to make a checklist to get everything organized for the wedding. Scrambling around her room, she looked for a spare piece of paper to write on. After giving up, she used her phone and opened a new note. She titled it: *Things to Do Before I Get Married.*

"Well, those are words I didn't think I'd be writing this week," Kylee muttered out loud to herself.

She started listing things out.

1.) Pack up clothes and stuff
2.) Find a wedding dress
3.) Find birth certificate

She thought about what else she needed to do. If this were her real wedding, she'd probably have a never-ending list. Getting her nails done, booking her hair and makeup, shoe shopping, checking on floral arrangements, probably a bachelorette party...not to mention, she'd probably include her family in the events.

Not that there was much to them. Kylee was an only child. Her parents had managed to hold on to their rocky marriage until she was in high school before they finally divorced. It was sad, but she'd been expecting it for years. They hadn't exactly had a picture-perfect marriage. She'd still lived with her mom until she graduated, but considering her mom had emotionally checked out, Kylee was spurred into an early life of independence.

There hadn't been too many family get-togethers over the years. Kylee made sure to call them every few weeks just to stay in touch, though, and she definitely would have invited them to her wedding if it had actually been a real one.

She sighed and shook her head. This wasn't a real wedding. Her parents didn't need to know about the reckless thing she was about to do. She just had to get the basics done.

Kylee set her phone down and decided to jump in the shower. She still had her shift at the library this morning. Her two-day-a-week position as a library clerk was a nice supplement to her freelance designing. Although, "library clerk" was a nice way of saying she reshelved books for about six hours. It wasn't glamorous, but it helped pay the bills.

After getting dressed, she walked out to the kitchen. Elena was eating a bowl of cereal at the table.

"Good morning, sunshine," her roommate said as she scooped another bite of Cheerios into her mouth. "What are you going to do on your last day of freedom? You know, before the old ball and chain happens?"

Kylee rubbed her eyes. "Tell me again why I'm agreeing to this?"

Elena winked. "Because Ryan is an extremely attractive man, and you're hoping this fake marriage will turn into a real one in the end."

Kylee snagged a few stray Cheerios on the counter and chucked them at her roommate. "I am not! I'm only doing this because Ryan is my good friend." She shrugged. "And he offered to pay off my school debt. His looks have absolutely nothing to do with it."

"Of course they don't. I know you're not that shallow." Elena gave her an innocent look.

"Okay, enough joking. Seriously, what are you going to do today? Do you need help with anything?"

Kylee shrugged. "I don't know. I need to pack up enough clothes to last me a few weeks at Ryan's place. I figure I'll be back in a month, so no sense in moving everything. I also probably need to find a dress to get married in. He'll probably want to take a picture or two for evidence, so I better look the part." She pulled a bowl out of the cabinet and poured herself some cereal. "I have my shift at the library this morning and one or two things I have to finish editing this afternoon, though."

"So you're really staying at his place?"

She shrugged as she added milk to her bowl. "I mean, we're technically supposed to be married. What if one of his family members or friends comes to visit? That would probably look a little weird if I wasn't there." Kylee had been to Ryan's place a couple of times. Once to watch the Nuggets in a playoff game the year before, and another time for a Fourth of July barbecue. She'd had no problem hanging out at his place as a friend before. But she knew it'd be totally different going there as his wife.

Elena got up and put her empty bowl into the sink. "Well, even though this isn't your *real* wedding, we need to do something fun. Let's go dress and accessory shopping tonight. I'm off work at six. Can we go then?"

"Yeah? That'd be great, let's do it." Kylee smiled to herself. No, it wasn't necessary, but why not have a little fun with the situation? It couldn't hurt to live up the moment a little.

"We can think of it as your bachelorette party. Maybe we'll go crazy and get our nails done."

Kylee snorted and put her arm around Elena. "I don't know what I'm going to do without you for the next few weeks!"

"You'll just have to spend your days looking at Ryan's mug instead of this beautiful face!" she answered, batting her eyelashes.

"I don't know how I'll survive," Kylee responded dryly as Elena walked off. A sudden surge of nerves filled her at the thought, though. A whole month of living with Ryan. How would she ever keep her feelings at bay for that long?

# Chapter 3

Ryan had been going nonstop all day. He'd been back and forth on the phone with his brother, Mason, half the morning, confirming everything was in place as far as the trust was concerned. Mason had met with the family attorney, Frank, that morning. Frank was their grandpa's trustee. If anyone knew the ins and outs of the trust stipulations, it was him.

Then, there were all the things he needed to get done for the wedding. The *fake* wedding. That differentiation needed to be stressed.

Getting all the marriage license paperwork had taken up the rest of the morning. He'd then spent the early afternoon cleaning out the spare bedroom. Ryan decided he would sleep in the spare room so Kylee could have his room while she was there. It would be an inconvenience to go from a king-sized, gel-cushioned bed with a pillow-top layer to a twin-size air mattress. But apparently, even fake marriages required some sacrifice.

Now, he was on his way to a department store to buy a realistic-looking, fake diamond ring. He figured a good cubic zirconia would be worth it for a few weeks.

His phone buzzed on the passenger seat next to him. It was his brother, Mason. Ryan hit "accept" and the bluetooth on his car picked up the call.

"Hey, dude, what's up?"

"I'm over here slaving away for you," Mason said. "That's what's up."

"I know. I owe you one. What'd you find out?"

"So, I didn't catch all his legal jargon, but I think everything is as you thought. According to Frank, it takes the system around seventy-two hours to process and formally acknowledge your marriage as legit. Once that's done, the money can be transferred to you."

Ryan breathed a sigh of relief. "Awesome. Whew. Thanks, bud." His bag manufacturer wouldn't start production until they had the payment transferred to them. The quicker he got that done, the quicker everything could get moving.

"Of course, if the marriage is found out to be fake or done purely for financial purposes, there will be ramifications later on."

Ryan sighed as he pulled up to a red light. He knew he could get in serious trouble if his true purposes were found out. "What kind of ramifications?"

"Frank was throwing around words like 'marriage fraud' and 'financial fraudulence'..." His voice trailed off for a moment. "Essentially, you just need to be sure you put on a good show for everyone."

Ryan tried to swallow the lump forming in his throat. "Well, fingers crossed Kylee's a good actress."

"Let's hope," his brother said ominously.

Ending the call, Ryan took a deep breath. This wasn't going to be a disaster. They'd get away with it. He'd get his company back on track, and in the process, he'd pay Kylee's student loans off. It would all be fine.

Wouldn't it?

*****

Somehow, Ryan made it to the department store ten minutes later, even with his mind a million miles away. Was he putting himself at risk with this plan? More importantly, was he putting Kylee at risk?

He chose to ignore the sour pit in his stomach. He'd push through and make sure nothing bad happened to either of them.

Ryan reached the jewelry counter and circled cluelessly for a few minutes before admitting he needed help. He found a woman who looked in charge, according to her all-black outfit and severely slicked-back hair.

"Excuse me." She looked up at him, a perfectly fake smile spreading across her face. "Hi, uh, I'm looking for the cubic zirconia rings." He waited for her look of dismay, but she didn't even blink.

"Yes, follow me. They're right over here." She led him to a large display he'd already passed, assuming they were diamond rings. "Here's our selection of some of the best cubic zirconia you'll find. And as you can see, their price points are quite affordable."

He was pleasantly surprised at how nice the rings looked. He would have never guessed they weren't the real thing—not that he knew anything about jewelry.

He eyed a single solitaire, knowing that Kylee would appreciate the simplicity.

Ryan had known Kylee for three years. Their friendship had begun when she freelanced a design project for him. A friend had recommended her graphic work, and she'd done a great job. From there, they had gotten to know each other little by little over the years. They met up for lunch, watched a few Nuggets games together, and they'd even worked together on a few more projects. Kylee had been the one to design the logo and website for Hudson's Packs. Somehow—almost without trying—they'd become quite close.

Kylee's style was simple. She'd never been one to dress with tons of accessories or all the extra frivolousness some girls did. As Ryan thought about it, he realized she took a simple, straightforward approach to most things in life. She'd never complicated things between them. Kylee seemed to take their friendship for exactly what it was, never once pressuring or hinting at anything serious.

But he'd gone and complicated it, hadn't he? He hoped that everything would go back to normal after this fake marriage was dealt with.

"Can I see that one?" he asked, motioning toward the solitaire.

"Of course." The woman laid the ring on top of the glass case for him to inspect.

He picked it up, looking at it from all angles. While he did, an overwhelming feeling hit him as he realized what he was doing.

Marriage. It was something he'd always thought of seriously. A lifetime commitment he'd only make once. Was he really going to do this? Even though it wasn't going to be a true marriage, the enormity of it made him freeze.

"I am sure the future owner of this ring will love it." The woman's voice brought him back to the present.

Yes, he was going to do this.

He smiled at her. "I hope you're right. I'll take it."

She nestled it in a velvet ring box before boxing the whole thing up. "Here you go, sir," she said, handing it over. "You can pay for it up front. Have a good day."

As he took it from her, an image of him putting the ring on Kylee's finger entered his mind, sending a flush of warmth through him. Did he actually like that idea?

No, he was being ridiculous.

He turned away from the jewelry counter. What had made him think of that? It wasn't like either one of them had actual romantic feelings for each other. She was just his friend, doing him a favor. That was all.

After paying for the ring at the front of the store, he left for his final errand: picking up a bouquet of flowers.

Ryan wasn't totally clueless. He knew getting married was an emotional thing for any woman, regardless if it was fake or not. Kylee would appreciate having flowers to hold. It didn't hurt that they'd make the pictures seem more realistic.

There was a small florist shop about a mile away. He assumed he could find something there on his way home.

When Ryan walked into the store, he was immediately greeted by an older woman who couldn't have been more than about five feet tall. Her bubbly personality more than made up for her lack of height, though.

"Good evening! Welcome, welcome, my name is Joan. What can I help you with today?" She had a stray flower petal stuck in her fluffy bun, and her apron was streaked with bright hues of green.

"Hi. I'm looking for a bouquet of flowers. Maybe something someone would hold when they're getting married?" He didn't want to come straight out and say he was getting a bouquet for his bride. That would have led to way too many questions.

"Oh, well, let's see. We have a few arrangements of roses—those would be the most traditional." She led him to a display case where there were a few premade bouquets, all in various colors of tight rosebuds.

"Hmm. I mean, these are pretty." He stroked his chin as he thought about Kylee. "I was hoping for something a little more unique." He didn't know why, but Kylee didn't feel like a rose kind of girl. She was more special than that.

"What kind of style does the recipient of the flowers like?"

"Style?"

"Yes," Joan said, nodding. "Does she have a flair to her, or does she tend more toward traditional fashions? Or does she love whimsical designs?" She waved her hands about dramatically as she spoke.

"Um, well, she usually seems to keep things simple...maybe...whimsical did you call it?" Ryan stammered, suddenly feeling out of his element.

"Never mind, never mind." She held her hands up once more to silence him. He swore he heard her mutter something about *men*. "Let's try a different approach. If she had to choose between a formal dinner and a casual barbecue, which would she choose?"

Ryan didn't hesitate before answering that. "Barbecue."

"Does she generally wear high heels or flats?"

"Flats."

"What is her favorite color?"

"I think purple. At least that's the color she wears the most."

"Does she wear her hair down or pulled up more often?"

"Down...like wavy and loose." Ryan twirled his fingers over his head to demonstrate.

Joan smiled at his antics. "And most importantly, what are you trying to get across with these flowers?"

"What do you mean by *get across*?"

"I mean, what's your purpose in them? Are these to show your love for her? Are they a bouquet of apology flowers? Are they flowers of friendship?"

"I...Well, they're just friendship flowers. Yes. Friendship. There's nothing, absolutely nothing, serious between us."

She eyed him, her hands folding slowly. "There's nothing between you and this woman, but you want a unique bouquet of flowers that someone might hold at a wedding and you seem quite confident in your knowledge about her?"

Was this lady a florist or a therapist?

"Er, yep," he managed to spit out around his swirling thoughts. "Just friends."

Right? Weren't they? Just friends doing each other a favor...by getting married?

That sounded ridiculous, even to him. But that was all they'd ever been. Friends. Sure, he knew a lot about her. He'd spent a lot of time with her. That was natural.

*Why hadn't anything ever happened between us?* he suddenly wondered in the back of his mind.

Joan, meanwhile, accepted his answer with a shrug. "Well, given your answers, I would definitely include some ranunculus flowers in your arrangement."

She walked as she spoke, and Ryan followed like a dog on a leash. She stopped in front of a bucket full of flowers with delicate, almost papery petals. The colors ranged from dark pink to a light coral. She took her time selecting four or five of the blooms, all of them a similar rose shade.

"We're also going to need some peonies, of course." She was almost talking to herself as she turned to another bucket full of a voluptuous flower in a pale pink. After she'd picked several of those, the bouquet began to take shape.

Next, she strode over to several pots filled with different green stems and leaves. Ryan couldn't make heads or tails of it, but apparently, there was a method to her madness. Three minutes later, she was holding one of the most beautiful floral arrangements he had ever seen.

"Wow, that looks…wow!"

"It is quite the thing, isn't it?" she said affectionately as she plucked a fallen leaf from her arm. "Wait, one more thing." She arranged two large, white flowers on opposite sides, balancing out the look. "Calla lilies seem like the perfect finishing touch."

Ryan paid for the bouquet a few minutes later and headed home. Once he'd walked in the door, he set his stuff down and slumped into a chair.

He was pretty sure he'd covered everything. He was planning on wearing a suit he had worn as one of the groomsmen for his cousin's wedding. Sure, it wasn't as formal as a tux, but the suit had been expensive and fit him better than any rental tux would, anyway.

He suddenly realized he hadn't talked to Kylee about what she was wearing. Ryan should probably call her and touch base before tomorrow.

After three rings, her phone went to voicemail. Her message—the one she hadn't changed in at least two years—played in his ears. "Hi, this is Kylee Morgan! Sorry I can't answer right now, but leave me a message, and I'll get back to you."

Before the beep could sound, he hung up and then sent her a text instead.

***Hey, Kylee. Just giving you an update for tomorrow. I've scheduled a 9 AM appointment at the courthouse. If you want, I can pick you up.***

He clicked send and leaned back into the couch. He grabbed the remote and flipped the channels until he hit ESPN. A few minutes later, his phone buzzed with a response.

***The groom isn't supposed to see the bride before the wedding.***

He chuckled and responded.

***I guess you're right. Okay then, I'll see you there.***

***Do you want me to bring my camera? I'm assuming you want evidence of our nuptials.***

Ryan planned to snap a few photos with his phone afterwards. He knew Kylee did a lot of photography for her design work, though, so she probably had a much better camera than him.

***Yeah, that'd be great. We'll want our grandkids to be able to see where it all started.***

Her reply to that was quick.

***You are ridiculous.***

*****

In the dressing room, Kylee smiled as she put down her phone.

"What are you grinning about?" Elena asked as she came back with more dresses.

Kylee bit back her smile. "Oh nothing. So what did you find?"

This was the third store they had stopped at on their wedding dress hunt. Kylee wanted something understated and casual. After all, this was a fake wedding. Elena insisted it had to, at least, be white.

Casual, white dresses were clearly not in high demand right now, due to the lack of options. They were making the best of it anyway.

"So, this one has a blue ribbon around the waist. However, I thought the silhouette would be perfect for you." Elena held up a slinky dress that was cut in a deep V-neck and had an extremely high hemline.

Kylee raised an eyebrow at her roommate. "Elena, we're shopping for me, not for you. While you could rock that dress with your Latina curves, I would feel like an exposed mouse."

Elena did a little shimmy with her shoulders. "Come on, Kylee!"

Kylee just crossed her arms.

Sighing, her roommate tossed the dress onto the pile of rejects. "Okay, I actually assumed you wouldn't go for that one. But this next one is a winner."

The second dress she held up was made of a white lace material. It had a high, eyelash lace neckline that tapered down to a fitted waist. It filled out to a delicate, midi-length skirt. The whole look was a very feminine, bohemian look.

"Oooh, yes," Kylee exclaimed.

"And the best part is," Elena added as Kylee grabbed the dress, "it's on sale!"

"Even better."

As Kylee stepped into the dress and slid it up her body, she knew this was the one.

Elena zipped up the back, letting out a sigh as she did. The dress fit Kylee like a glove, hugging all the right curves and angles. Kylee didn't have a very voluptuous figure, but this dress made her body feel perfect.

"I love it," she said as Elena squealed behind her. She twirled side to side, eyeing herself from all angles. She couldn't help wondering what Ryan's reaction would be when he saw her in this. Would he be stunned?

"*Ay*! It really is perfect for you. Now just imagine yourself holding a bouquet of flowers, staring into Ryan's eyes as you walk slowly down the aisle—er, well, I guess standing in front of the judge's desk. Is that where it happens?"

Kylee's momentary elation fell. She didn't know why she was so excited. This wasn't real. She wasn't marrying Prince Charming. This was just a business transaction.

"Yeah, something like that." She reached back and unzipped the dress, suddenly ready to be out of it.

Elena didn't seem to notice. "Do you have shoes to go with this?"

Kylee imagined which ones would match this dress the best. "I have a pair of nude flats I could wear."

"You can't wear flats to your wedding!" Elena exclaimed, which she followed with some muttering to herself in Spanish. "I have the perfect pair of heels you can wear. They might be a little big, but they'll have to do."

Elena's feet were about a half size bigger than Kylee's. But they swapped shoes enough to know that she could make it work. She smiled and nodded. It was nice to have her roommate's support, but it was becoming more than Kylee could bear when none of this was real.

Yeah, she was getting married tomorrow, but she wasn't walking down an aisle. She was going to say "I do," but it wasn't forever.

As they were checking out, Elena asked, "What else do you need to get or do before tomorrow?"

"I should probably finish packing. I also need to get my camera equipment together to take pictures." Kylee ran through a mental list of the things she needed.

"Pshh, that's not what I meant! Those things aren't important. I meant, do you want to get your nails done? Do we need to pick up any last-minute accessories? Do you know how you're doing your hair and makeup in the morning?"

Kylee simply shook her head. "Yes, for the most part. But I think you're forgetting that this is not a real wedding. The only reason this is happening is so Ryan can get the money to fund his business. He couldn't care less what his fake bride looks like."

Elena rolled her eyes. "Of course he cares!" Holding the door open, she continued. "Regardless if it's real or fake, you are his woman for the next month."

Kylee walked out of the store, the sky darkening as the sun set. It reminded her of how her life was darkening a little, becoming more complicated than just student loans and juggling jobs. This wedding—even though it was pretend—had started to become a bit of a dark spot, and the marriage hadn't even started.

"I think you're overestimating the future of this pretend marriage, Elena," Kylee finally responded.

Her friend stopped her in the middle of the parking lot and grabbed her hand. "And I think you're underestimating it."

# Chapter 4

Kylee's alarm buzzed loudly at 6 a.m. on her wedding day.

Her *wedding* day.

She sat up quickly at the thought, and her eyes caught the dress hanging on the door frame.

Her *wedding* dress.

She shook her head, willing herself to ignore the doubts in her mind. She had things to do—like get ready. Despite the fact that she'd told Elena she wasn't concerned about her appearance, she still planned to spend the next hour and a half primping.

After a quick rinse in the shower, she started on her hair. She decided to go simple with the style. She twisted her ash-blonde locks into an elegant, low bun, wanting it pulled back so as to emphasize the neckline detail of her dress. Then, she artfully pinned some pieces back, leaving a few strands to frame her face.

Satisfied, she moved on to her makeup. She got about ten minutes into her attempt at a smoldering eye before frustratingly scrubbing it all off.

"Elena!" she yelled, storming out of her room. She walked into her roommate's room without knocking.

Elena looked at her, bleary-eyed, over her blankets. "Is there a fire? Please tell me there is a life-threatening reason you're yelling at me this early," she said, her voice hoarse.

Kylee flipped on the light. "It's basically life-threatening. I need you to do my makeup for my wedding."

At the word *wedding,* Elena popped up, all signs of tiredness gone. "Well, why didn't you say so? Here, let's go into my office." She waved her hands dramatically toward her oversized vanity in the corner.

Kylee rolled her eyes as she followed. Elena was one of those people who loved playing around with makeup. After pulling Kylee down into the chair, she turned on the bright lights lining the vanity mirror. Immediately, Kylee's face was illuminated with light.

"Hmm, some darkness under the eyes... No serious complexion issues right now, though..." Elena spoke in a low voice as she turned Kylee's head from side to side. "We want you stunning but not in an over-the-top look. Obviously, we need to play up your eyes, but your lips are pretty *fantástico* too…" After another moment of silence, she said, "All right. I'm going to give you a classic uptown-girl look."

"What exactly is an uptown-girl look?" Kylee asked, doubt hinting in her voice.

Elena was already digging through her drawers. "Where did I put that new eyeshadow palette?" She haphazardly pulled items out and set them on the desk.

Foundation, powders, brushes... She had it all.

Using her heel, Elena spun Kylee's chair so she was facing the window, not the mirror. "I want this to be a surprise, so no peeking."

Kylee let out the breath she'd been holding. "Okay, I trust you. Make me beautiful."

"Well, you already are beautiful," Elena said automatically, ever the loyal friend. She pulled out some foundation and began dabbing spots on Kylee's face. "This is just going to enhance it."

She worked intently for another twenty minutes, sometimes explaining what she was doing, other times working in silence. When she finally pulled back, she studied her creation.

"My goodness! I don't want to toot my own horn, but girl. You. Are. Smoldering." She emphasized each word with a flick of her makeup brush. "Ryan's got to be the luckiest fake groom that ever walked this planet."

Kylee spun to face the mirror. A hand flew to her face as she took in the person in front of her. She really did look beautiful. As Elena had said, she'd simply enhanced all of Kylee's natural features. Her high cheekbones had an attractive pink flush to them, and her skin looked dewy and fresh. Her lips shone with a nude gloss, but the star was definitely her eyes. Elena had played up their natural, green color with a subtle lavender eyeshadow. And she had somehow made her eyelashes look a million miles long.

"Elena, I don't know what to say. You're a master!"

"I know," her roommate responded humbly.

"No, but seriously, if you didn't make so much money as a pharmacist, I would say you need to switch careers." Kylee tilted her head from side to side, still inspecting the look.

"I do like what you've done with your hair—simple but elegant." Elena tucked in a stray piece. "What time are you planning on leaving?"

Kylee checked the time. "I have about ten minutes." That would give her twenty minutes to make their 9 a.m. appointment.

"Here." Elena went to her closet, scrambling inside for a moment. When she emerged, she was carrying a pair of nude, slingback heels, a splattering of crystals on the toes. "These shoes will go perfect with your dress." She held the shoes up, a frown creasing her lips. "They'll probably be a little big, though… Maybe we can stuff the toes with socks."

"It's like you're my fairy godmother," Kylee replied, taking the shoes from her.

"Just, with me, the clock doesn't stop at midnight."

Kylee smiled. She slipped the shoes on and stood, admiring them in the mirror. "They are perfect!" she exclaimed as she took a step forward before promptly falling flat on her face. "Uh, I think you may be right about the too big part, though."

After a few minutes of attempting to get the fit right with a spare pair of Elena's socks, Kylee gave up.

"I love the shoes, but it's not worth twisting my ankle for them. I'll just wear the flats I initially planned on. The dress is so long you won't even see my feet anyway."

Elena mumbled something in Spanish under her breath but shrugged her agreement as Kylee slipped out to go get dressed.

Ten minutes later, she came back, striking a dramatic pose for Elena's sake.

Her roommate clapped her hands with glee. "Oh, Kylee, you're gorgeous. Absolutely gorgeous!"

Kylee did a little twirl. "Last chance to stop me. Is this crazy to go through with it?"

A serious look came over Elena's face. "If you don't do it, you'll always wonder what might have happened if you had."

Kylee nodded and shouldered the camera bag she'd left next to the couch. "Okay, then. Wish me luck."

"*Buena suerte, amiga.*"

As Kylee walked to her car, though, she wondered if she'd need more than that *buena suerte* after she said "I do" to Ryan.

*****

It was 9:05. Was Kylee planning on standing Ryan up? Even though the marriage wasn't technically real, the thought hurt.

Just as Ryan was getting ready to call her, a stunning woman in a white dress came around the corner. The white dress she was wearing masterfully fit her body, somehow both clinging to it and floating away from it at all the right places. The woman was absolutely stunning. Everything about her seemed like perfection.

It was only when he finally focused on her face that he realized he was staring at Kylee.

*What the...*

Not that he didn't think Kylee was attractive—because she was, in a pretty, friend kind of way—but she was putting off a whole different kind of vibe today.

It was only when she cocked an eyebrow at him that he realized he'd been staring with wide eyes and an open mouth.

He tried to pull himself together. "Kylee, you look…well…wow! I mean..." He was stuttering like a fool. Not knowing what else to do, he shoved the bouquet of flowers at her with as much grace as a goat. "Here, I got you these. I figured a bride better have some flowers, right?"

The puzzlement in her eyes dissolved when she looked down at the flowers. "Oh my gosh, these are beautiful."

She buried her face in the delicate blooms and inhaled. "I don't think I've ever seen such a pretty arrangement."

Her genuine pleasure gave Ryan all sorts of uncomfortable, warm feelings.

"It was nothing. Just from a flower shop around the corner." For some unknown reason, he was trying to downplay the gesture.

She just smiled. "This wasn't nothing. Thank you so much."

Her smile, however, only managed to draw his attention to her lips and how soft they currently looked. He found himself wondering what it'd be like to kiss them. He quickly offered her his arm, needing to move on from this moment. "Well," he stammered, clearing his throat, "are you ready?"

Uncertainty flashed in her eyes at the change of subject. It was so quick that he almost missed it. But it had been there.

She threw her shoulders back. "Let's do this." She tucked her hand in the crook of his elbow, its warmth somehow comforting.

They walked to the front desk, where one of the secretaries helped them finish the paperwork for the marriage license. They both had to sign a few dotted lines and show their IDs before Ryan paid the fee.

After that, they were ushered into an open room with rows of benches. They were divided down the middle by an aisle, large windows bordering one side. The front contained nothing but a wide walkway leading to two doors on either side. Ryan wondered if this was where the marriages were performed. Was this a whole Kylee-walking-down-the-aisle sort of thing? He'd assumed they'd just get married in a side office or something.

The woman helping them said they could wait here for their name to be called. After a brief smile, she turned and returned to the front office area.

Ryan let Kylee lead the way toward one of the benches in the front. He sat down next to her, aware of the extra foot of space he'd put between them. He'd have to stop doing things like that once they were married. People would think it was odd if they were so distant with each other.

Kylee gazed down at her flowers, absentmindedly playing with the stems that had been wrapped in a thick satin ribbon. He studied her profile, wondering what she was thinking. When he noticed the pearl drop earrings she had in her ears, he realized he'd never said anything about her appearance except an oafish "Wow!" She must have gone through a lot of work this morning, and he hadn't even complimented her.

"You look beautiful, by the way."

Her eyes opened wide as she turned toward him. "What?"

"I said, you look beautiful. I've never seen you so..." He waved his hands at her. "Dolled up. It's nice. You really look amazing."

She began to blush.

Hoping he hadn't embarrassed her, he quickly added, "Not that I don't think you normally look nice!"

She just smiled at him, and he couldn't help noticing how the rosy flush had enhanced her features. "Thank you. I figured I'd better put in the extra effort for my wedding day."

A knot formed in his throat when he thought about that. This was her wedding day. He tried to swallow the lump, but the fact that he was tainting what should have been the most important day of her life made his stomach churn. Why hadn't he thought about that before he'd asked her?

He was about to respond when another couple came into the room. They weren't dressed quite as formally as Ryan and Kylee were. The woman was wearing a simple sundress, and the man had on slacks and an open-collared shirt. But they looked giddy with excitement.

Such a stark contrast to how quiet and uncomfortable he and Kylee were.

Ryan ran his hands along the edge of the wooden bench. His mind was blank, and he couldn't think of a single thing to say to the woman he was about to marry. Luckily, the 9 a.m. slot was the first of the day, so they should be called soon.

Just as he was beginning to tap his toes, a man in a dark suit entered through a door at the front of the room."Ryan Hudson and Kylee Morgan?"

It was showtime.

*****

Kylee stood stiffly, barely even noticing when Ryan reached back for her hand. The gesture should have surprised her, considering the five feet of space he'd placed between them on the bench.

Feeling as if she were walking in a dream, she followed Ryan to the front. This was it. She was about to pledge herself to a man under pretense of a business arrangement. A man that had no idea she had genuine feelings for him. The flowers that had brought her so much joy a few minutes ago felt like lead in her hand.

The man who'd called their name motioned them out the door and down a hallway. The small room they entered a minute later had a desk in the center. Inside, the man closed the door and motioned for them to sit in the two available chairs.

"Welcome. Congratulations on your decision to get married!" he said. When he grinned, the solemn feeling in the room suddenly lightened. "I'm Judge Caldwell. I will be your officiant today." He looked at the sheet of paper he had in his hands. "Were there any special requests? And are we using the standard vows, or did you write your own?"

Kylee glanced over at Ryan, who shrugged his shoulders.

“No special requests. Just the normal proceedings will be fine.” Ryan gave her hand a squeeze.

“All right. Then we’ll just get started. If you would both come stand in front of me?”

The ceremony was the fastest five minutes of Kylee’s life. The whole thing was basically a blur. When the judge eventually turned to her, she repeated the final words robotically.

“I, Kylee Morgan, take thee, Ryan Hudson…” She looked into his eyes, and the emotion in them caused her to stumble. Was that fear she saw? Or something else? “T-to be my wedded husband...” She somehow managed to make it through the vows by keeping her eyes focused on Ryan’s tie instead of his eyes.

“Are you exchanging rings today?” The judge’s question jolted Kylee.

She hadn’t even thought about rings. Had Ryan? When she lifted her eyebrows, Ryan momentarily dropped her hands.

“Uh, yeah, I have them—right here.” He fumbled in his pockets before coming out with a set of two rings. One was a simple, thick band, but the other was a delicate diamond solitaire.

Kylee stared at it in shock. It couldn’t have been real, right? There was no way Ryan had gotten her a real diamond ring for this wedding.

Ryan took her left hand, separating her third finger from the rest. She was surprised to feel his hands shaking slightly as he slid the ring down her finger.

"I hope it fits," he said in a low voice. "I had to guess on the size."

She wiggled her finger. The ring slid a little; it was probably half a size off. "Pretty close."

He smiled and placed the simple band in her hand. She stared at it, not sure what to do for a second.

"Oh," she said quietly. She was supposed to put this on *his* finger. She grabbed his hand and awkwardly slid the circle on it. Her fingers almost felt numb with nerves, and she felt like someone ought to have given her an award for not dropping the thing.

"Excellent!" the judge said as they finished with the rings. "Now, with the power vested in me, by the state of Colorado, I pronounce you husband and wife." He beamed at them. "You may kiss the bride!"

If Kylee thought she'd been nervous before, that was nothing compared to the explosion of butterflies that rocked her. She'd forgotten about the whole "kiss the bride" part.

She wouldn't admit it out loud, but she'd imagined kissing Ryan before. She'd imagined him softly brushing a stray strand of hair from her face, then freezing as he gazed into her eyes, for the first time realizing the feelings he had for her. Then, overcome with his passion, he'd swoop her up into his arms. Without control, their lips would meet and—

Her daydream was interrupted when real-life Ryan grabbed one of her hands. She stared down at their linked fingers, trying to decide if that cold, clammy feeling was coming from his hand or hers. It wasn't until he'd pulled her close, their faces inches apart, that she realized this was actually happening.

Ryan Hudson was about to kiss her.

She had a split second to gaze into his dark eyes, not exactly sure what she saw in them, before his lips were on hers.

What began as a firm kiss instantly melted into something soft. She responded immediately, surprising herself. His mouth was warm and inviting, and it caused everything else to fade away. She felt his solid arm behind her, not allowing her to move back an inch even if she'd wanted to. An unknown sense told her to pull him tighter as his clean scent washed over her.

Suddenly, he pulled back, and she was staring into eyes that looked as shocked as she felt. Neither one of them had moved, their bodies still inches apart.

"Congratulations, you two!"

The booming voice made them jump, the distance between them doubling. Ryan's hands flew to his sides, and Kylee began nervously twisting the ring that felt so out of place on her finger.

"If you just head back toward the front office, they'll have your paperwork all ready for you. I wish you both happiness in your new life." The judge's smile was bright and friendly, but it was clear his work was done.

Kylee picked up the bouquet she'd set on the chair and followed Ryan out the door. Following behind them, the judge strode off toward the main room, ready to tie the knot for another couple.

"Well," Kylee said, keeping her gaze focused on a light freckle near Ryan's nose instead of the mouth she'd just explored, "I guess it's done now."

Ryan smiled, although she noticed his face still seemed a little flush. "May I have the honor of being the first to address you as Mrs. Hudson?"

She slapped him lightly on the shoulder, never more grateful for his sense of humor than at that moment. "You're such a dork. I expect you to solely address me as 'darling' or 'my dear' from now on." Then, she tapped her chin with her flowers. "Though I will also accept 'Your Majesty.'"

He laughed. "All right. Let's go get this paperwork."

They made their way down the hallway to the front office area. There, a woman had them sign out before wishing them good luck with everything.

Kylee passed through the door Ryan held open for her, the crisp morning air filling her lungs. She glanced around, taking note of the few people walking or driving by. Was it just another Friday morning for all of them? Did any of them make a life-changing commitment like her today?

"We should probably take a picture," Ryan said as he stepped out beside her. "We might want to frame one and put it on our mantel or something."

She gave him a half smile. "I left my camera stuff in my car. We can go get it and snap a few photos."

He nodded and followed her to the parking lot.

*****

Wow. That kiss was not what Ryan had expected.

Not at all.

Not that he'd expected Kylee to be a bad kisser or anything. He just hadn't expected to feel such a connection with her. He hadn't expected that spark. If anything, he was expecting things to be awkward and stiff. Clearly, he'd been wrong. Only knowing that the judge had been standing a foot away had given him the awareness to finally pull back.

He followed Kylee from behind, noticing the way her hips swayed with every step. He shook himself mentally and took a quick step so he was walking beside her instead. There. Much safer.

If there was one thing he couldn't do during this whole fake marriage, it was develop feelings for Kylee.

Not that he was concerned. He and Kylee had had a great friendship over the last few years. But that was all it was: a friendship. Definitely not one he wanted to put in jeopardy for a few extra kisses.

No matter how right the first one had felt.

When they reached her car, Kylee pulled out a small duffel bag and folded tripod.

"I brought the tripod," she said. "I figured it would be more reliable than asking strangers to take a photo for us."

"Smart thinking. Where do you think is the best photo op?" He would let her take the reins on this one. He knew next to nothing about photography.

"Let's go back to the front steps of the courthouse. I think it will create a good frame for a picture."

Ryan shouldered the bag and indicated for Kylee to hand him the tripod as well.

In front of the courthouse building, Kylee hummed for a minute. She eventually took the tripod from Ryan and set it up directly in front of the steps. Next, she removed a wide camera lens from her bag. Ryan watched as she fumbled around with the settings, completely lost in her work.

He couldn't help but enjoy watching Kylee, his new wife, working so seriously.

"Can you stand on the steps for a second?" she asked. "I need a figure to focus on."

Ryan positioned himself on the steps, moving left a few feet then back right as per her hand gestures. He struck a few comical poses, getting some giggles out of Kylee as she peered through the camera lens.

"Will you hold still?!" she demanded as she tried to bite back a smile. "I'm trying to focus things."

Ryan finally stopped his antics and shoved his hands inside his pockets. "This is my best look, anyway. It'll be on the cover of *Outdoor Life* one day," he announced. "Make sure you're getting my good side."

She ignored him and finally stood, satisfied with her setup. "All right. I think I have everything perfect." She walked next to him, pausing about a foot away. "How do you want to do this?" She looked uncertain about where to stand.

Ryan pulled her close, something he'd wanted to do again since their kiss. He tried to focus on the soft feeling of the lace on her dress instead of the warmth radiating from her skin. "Here, you stand next to me like this." He positioned her so she was facing him and their arms were around each other. "Do you have a remote, or is this thing on a timer?"

She twirled a remote in front of his face. "Remote. I'm just going to start clicking away, so make sure you're looking happy."

"That shouldn't be too hard," he mumbled under his breath.

She cocked an eyebrow but didn't respond. Then, she proceeded to click the shutter button with the rapidfire over the next thirty seconds. These photos would be proof of his happy marriage, so he might as well put on a good show.

Leaning down, he gave her a kiss on the cheek. When she looked at him in surprise, he swooped her up in his arms, winning him a loud shriek.

“What are you doing? Put me down,” she halfheartedly demanded through her laughs. She threw her arms around his neck in spite of her protests.

“I sure hope you’re actually getting photos of this,” he moaned, pretending to stagger.

“Put me down! I’m way too heavy for you,” she cried out again.

Laughing, he straightened with ease. “Kylee, you weigh basically nothing, and if you keep complaining, I’m going to carry you like this all the way home.”

She rolled her eyes. “Okay. Smile and I’ll take one. Then you’ll put me down.”

As she said, the lens opened and closed one more time on their smiling faces. Then, Ryan lowered her slowly to the ground.

“Do you think those are enough, or do we need another shot?” he asked. Not that he would have minded taking more posed photos with her. Having her in his arms certainly wasn’t a burden.

Kylee wanted to do one more location. This one went quicker, mostly because Ryan managed to simply stand in one place and smile this time.

By the time they made it back to the car, it was almost 10:30.

“You want to stop and get some breakfast?” Ryan asked as he stashed her bag in the back seat. “I didn’t eat anything this morning, so I’m starving.”

"I'm pretty hungry, too. What are you thinking?" Kylee responded.

"Burgers?"

She snorted. "I thought you said you wanted breakfast."

"Yeah, well, burgers are basically like a breakfast sandwich—with lettuce and tomato. French fries are basically hash browns, and if you drink lemonade, you're essentially drinking the lemon version of orange juice."

Kylee's snort turned into full-blown laughter. Ryan loved that he had caused it.

"Okay, Mr. Nutritionist. How about you just lead the way, and I'll follow you?"

Ryan smiled as he opened her door. "I got a place you're going to love."

*****

Kylee followed as Ryan led them to what looked like a truck stop called Pete's Burgers. The tagline alone had her rolling her eyes. The giant *"If it ain't beef, it ain't meat!"* sign was obnoxiously large across the front window.

Ryan got out of his car, grinning.

"Where did you find this place?" she asked as she walked over to him.

"A buddy of mine introduced me to it a couple years ago. I haven't been here in forever, though." He turned toward the giant sign. "They could work on their marketing, but I promise their burgers are actually amazing."

Twenty minutes later, they were sitting in a booth with hot food in front of them. Even Kylee had to admit he'd been right. The food was delicious.

She played with a french fry, stealthily admiring Ryan while he ate. He looked amazing in his suit. It must have been tailored, because it fit him perfectly.

"What are you thinking about?"

His comment made her drop the french fry she'd been holding. "Um, well, I was just thinking about how nice you look in your suit today. I've never seen you so dressed up. It looks good on you." Her traitorous cheeks began to flush. Why was she being so weird? She'd never had a problem being around Ryan before.

But before, they hadn't been married.

She mentally shook her head. Nothing had seriously changed. She could still be herself around him.

"Thanks," Ryan answered back. "I figured a tux would be a little over the top, so the suit had to do."

She just nodded.

"So," Ryan said, changing gears, "let's talk about what's next for us."

"What, like two and a half kids and a white picket fence?" Kylee quipped back.

"I mean, I appreciate your commitment to our image, but I'm not sure we need to go that far." The corners of his mouth lifted in an adorable smile. It was the same one she'd fallen for in the first place.

Her mouth was dry as she asked, "Okay, what's the plan?"

All seriousness now, he pulled his phone out of his pocket and scrolled through what appeared to be a list. "So, today, we need to get you settled into my place. We can stop by your apartment, and I can help load up whatever it is you're bringing. Then, we need to make a trip to see my family next week. This is kind of the main event." He set his phone on the table. "I, uh... I don't want to make you nervous, but that's where we really have to sell this whole marriage thing." He ran his fingers through his hair.

"So, what exactly are you planning on telling your family? I'm assuming they are going to be a little upset when they find out they missed their son's wedding." Kylee hadn't really worried about her own family's reaction to missing the wedding, because she never planned on telling them. If things went smoothly, her life would be back to normal in a month, her parents none the wiser. Ryan's family was another story.

"Well…" Ryan drawled out the word. "I was thinking I'd just tell them we were so in love we couldn't wait any longer." He looked at her with raised eyebrows. "I was also hoping you could play it off that you don't like big events. That the idea of a huge family wedding was just too overwhelming. That a small, courthouse wedding was what we both wanted?" His tone lifted in a question at the last word.

Kylee bit her lip. It wasn't the most convincing explanation, but she couldn't think of anything better herself. "I mean, obviously, your love for me couldn't be contained," she said, quickly taking a sip of her drink to hide her grin.

"Well, obviously—"

"And convincing everyone I don't like huge events where I'm the center of attention shouldn't be hard," she continued before he could quip back, "considering it's actually true. How long will we be visiting?"

"I thought we'd leave here Tuesday or Wednesday and come back Sunday. My aunt and uncle will be in town on Thursday, so my mom is planning a small family reunion."

Kylee set her cup back down. "Do you mind leaving on Wednesday? I work at the library on Tuesdays and Thursdays. I could probably get someone to cover for me Thursday, but I'd feel bad leaving both days on such short notice."

"Deal. We'll leave Wednesday morning. That'll be better anyway. Less time to be scrutinized by everyone. I'm sure there will be plenty of questioning from everyone once they find out."

That thought made Kylee's stomach swirl.

Ryan didn't seem to notice her sudden discomfort. "I'm actually a little nervous about the whole thing myself. I'm just worried that if my grandma finds out about this, she'll be ticked enough to stop the money transfer." He glanced at her, and she hoped he hadn't noticed how the color had drained from her face. "I'm sure everything will be fine, though. Really, don't stress about it at all," he hurriedly said.

So much for him not noticing. The burger in front of her didn't sound appealing anymore. Having to sell this to Ryan's family felt like more pressure than she could handle. She already had more than friendly feelings for him, but acting like a real couple in front of his relatives…

That could get messy.

*****

Kylee drove slower than usual because Ryan was following behind her in his car. But that was fine. It gave her more time alone to think.

Ryan mentioned that his brother, Mason, actually knew about the whole scheme, but other than that, no one was aware of what they'd just done.

She thought back over the last three hours. Her favorite part had to have been Ryan's face when he'd first seen her. Even though she was sure he'd never thought of her in a romantic way, the look of shock and interest his face had portrayed was flattering. The dress had worked its magic.

Taking pictures afterwards had actually been kind of fun. Ryan was good at keeping things light and carefree.

Even their lunch afterwards had been comfortable and relaxed. So far, the bulk of their three-hour marriage had been quite enjoyable.

The one moment she purposely avoided thinking about was that kiss.

*That kiss.*

The feeling of being in Ryan's arms, completely captivated by him, was something she didn't want to think about. Yet, she also didn't want to forget it.

She sighed and turned up the music. She had to get away from her feelings.

Too bad that'd be especially difficult come Wednesday.

Five minutes later, they pulled into the parking lot of her apartment. Kylee hopped out of her car and approached the door as Ryan walked over. The material of his dark suit laid perfectly across his broad shoulders, then came to a relaxed fit at his waist. He really was the perfect groom.

Watching him meant she wasn't watching where she was going, though. When she reached the curb, instead of stepping up like she should have, her foot barreled into the hard pavement. With a quick yelp, she began falling to her knees.

Luckily, Ryan reached forward and caught her at the last minute. Warmth flooded her face as she grabbed hold of the solid arm around her waist.

"Whoa!" he said, his voice low and directly behind her ear. "You okay?"

Absently, she nodded, but the only other thing she could do was breathe shallowly as his arm held her steady. Something about his closeness made her heart race.

She blinked hard and straightened herself. Turning, she gave him a brief smile. "Yeah, I'm fine, thanks."

Stiffly, she turned back toward the apartments, being sure to watch where she stepped this time. When they finally reached apartment 106, she reached for the door handle and unlocked it. She hoped Ryan hadn't noticed that it took her two tries to get the key in the lock with her sweaty palms.

Her apartment was empty. Elena was most likely at work since it was the middle of a Friday. In the main entryway sat Kylee's two suitcases.

Ryan followed her silently, his presence simultaneously comforting and nerve-racking.

"I didn't go crazy with my packing," she told him. "I assumed I could come back and pick up anything I forgot later on."

"Well, this will be easy then." He popped up the handle of one of the suitcases and threw the other over his shoulder.

"I can help with one of those," she said, reaching for the handle.

"No way. I'm the man in this relationship. I'll do the grunt work." He grinned, but he still didn't give up either suitcase.

"All right, tough guy," she teased, secretly appreciating his courtesy. "If you insist."

She let Ryan walk out first so she could lock up. Before she did, she stopped and turned to look at her apartment one more time. Was she really leaving this place? It wasn't permanent, but there was something scary about what she was doing.

Kylee looked over her shoulder at Ryan, who was standing outside the front door. He had a relaxed stance, and his face showed no signs of impatience. And suddenly, her doubts faded away, because this was Ryan, after all. He would always take care of her. She had nothing to worry about.

She stepped outside and closed the door with a firm yank. "All right. I'm ready."

*****

When they finally reached Ryan's condo, it was his turn to feel nervous. Was Kylee going to be comfortable at his place? He'd tried to make his room void of any personal effects. He wanted her to feel like that was her space while she lived there. But was it enough? He pulled her suitcases out of his trunk, still surprised that she had packed so little. But Kylee was never one for overdoing things.

He messed with his lock for a second, jiggling his key until he heard the click. Then, he gazed over his shoulder at her. "I'll have to get you a key made. I didn't think of that."

"You mean you're not going to keep me locked in your dungeon while I'm here?" Kylee asked with a wink.

"Only if you eat my secret stash of Doritos."

"Oooh, you'd better hide those good then." She grinned broadly. "It looks like we're going to have to make a list of house rules for each other. My pet peeve is people who leave dishes in the sink."

"What if I plan on washing them later?" he asked.

She folded her arms over her chest. "You never will. That's just a lie people who leave dishes in the sink tell themselves."

He laughed and shuffled in with the suitcases. When he turned around, Kylee was just about to step through the door herself. He realized the opportunity he was missing.

"Wait, stop!" he called out.

She froze, wide-eyed.

He briskly walked toward her and, before she could protest, swooped her up into his arms. "We all know I need to carry you across the threshold, right?" he said over her yelp of surprise.

She had wrapped her arms around his neck, probably more as a survival instinct than anything else, but he couldn't help liking the feeling. This was the second time in less than an hour he'd held her in his arms, and he couldn't understand why it'd taken him three years to do it. She felt so right and comfortable there. Both of them had been laughing as he walked through the doorway, but the moment their eyes locked, there was something besides humor between them. Something electric.

Ryan's gaze dropped to her lips. Then, realizing the dangerous situation he was putting them in, he set her down just as quickly as he had picked her up.

"Well, how about I show you your room," he said, no longer able to meet her eyes.

"Uh, yeah, that'd be great."

What was going on between them? They kept having these weird moments all morning where everything seemed to come to a halt. He needed to pull himself together.

He ran a hand over his eyes. It must have been the stress of getting married. There were too many emotions in the air; he couldn't think straight.

"You've been here before," he said as they walked through the main living area, "so I won't give you the grand tour. But feel free to make yourself at home." He glanced at the room, trying to see it from her eyes. An oversized couch took up the bulk of it, and there was a solid wooden coffee table in the middle. A huge TV was the main focus on one wall. He looked at his sad excuse for a houseplant sagging in the corner of the room. It was definitely a guy's place, but what could he have done about that?

"Yes, I was here during the final game of the playoffs last year," Kylee said, spinning around to get a look at the whole room.

"Ah, yes, when the Celtics beat us at the buzzer," he moaned. That had been a downer of a night. "Well, then yes, things haven't changed much since then." He glanced around one more time. "If you feel like you need to add something to give it a more homey touch, you have free reign." He held up one finger. "Except, I can't deal with any pink or purple decor in my house."

"How do you feel about sparkles?" she asked with a straight face.

Ryan just gave her a hard stare. Kylee broke out into laughter as she followed him to the hallway.

His office was the first room, the slightly ajar door giving them a good view of the mess inside. He cleared his throat as he reached out to shut it. "This will be my room while you're here. I moved most of my stuff out of the master bedroom yesterday. I haven't had time to organize everything in this room yet, though."

"You didn't need to move all your stuff for me," Kylee exclaimed, waving her hand at the closed door. "I could've slept there."

Ryan firmly shook his head. "I'm not going to have you sleeping on an air mattress in my spare bedroom, Kylee. You get the real bed. You're the one doing me the favor."

With that, he walked a few steps to the next door and opened it. "Is, uh…is this all okay?" he asked, hoping his insecurity wasn't totally obvious. He'd tried to make sure this room was clean. There were even fresh sheets and blankets on the bed.

“Yes, this is great. Thank you. But I do feel bad that you’re giving up your bedroom for me,” she answered as she studied the space.

“Well, I feel bad that I asked you to pretend to marry me,” he said, stepping aside so she could enter it.

“Touché,” she said.

Her smile had faltered for a moment, though, and he wished he could have taken back the comment. Apparently, she didn’t want to be reminded about the falsehood of their situation. He stepped out of the room. “Unfortunately, there’s only one bathroom, so we’ll have to share.” He indicated the third door down the hall. “I’ll let you have first dibs on it every morning, though.”

“You’re such a courteous husband. Maybe I’ll even leave you some hot water every day,” she said, batting her eyelashes.

“This must be true love,” he quipped back.

She smiled. “Thank you for making me comfortable here. I really do appreciate it.”

“Anything for you, dear.” He winked at her.

“Anything?” She widened her eyes. “Well, in that case, can you bring my suitcases back here for me?”

He sighed loudly as he walked down the hallway. “No one told me marriage would be this much work.”

“You’d better be careful,” Kylee called down to him. “Pretty soon, I’ll be making you a Honey-Do list.”

The thought made him laugh.

# Chapter 5

It had been at least six hours since Kylee had officially moved in, and Ryan still couldn't settle down. He chalked it up to a normal reaction to having someone else in his house, but it was more than that. It was *Kylee*. He hadn't been able to squash these bizarre feelings of attraction for her that he'd been getting since their kiss. And it was putting him on edge.

This wasn't supposed to happen. This was supposed to be a total business arrangement. Nothing more.

The whole carrying-her-over-the-threshold thing had probably crossed the line. Sure, Ryan had been trying to lighten the mood with the gesture, but he would have been lying if he didn't admit he'd wanted to feel her in his arms again.

He leaned back in his chair, rolling his neck slowly. The early afternoon had been a little awkward, neither one of them knowing what to do. Kylee had finally decided to go on a run about an hour ago, and he'd decided to work on some budget forecasts for Hudson's Packs. However, he'd spent the last thirty minutes staring at the same numbers with no progress. He just couldn't get his mind to settle down.

He glanced around the messy office/temporary bedroom and wondered if he should finish organizing it. Just as he decided to get back to his numbers, his cell buzzed with a new text. He picked up the phone and saw his brother Mason's name on the screen.

***How's married life? The wifey making you dinner right now?***

He rolled his eyes before responding.

***Yes, as a matter of fact, she's also ironing my shirts and vacuuming the house. You should get yourself a wife too.***

***No way, man. There are still too many girls out there for me to chain myself to just one.***

Ryan shoved his phone to the side. He actually shared his brother's sentiments—or he used to. Why settle down with just one woman when there were so many others out there? But for some reason, the thought of even flirting with another woman right now held no enticement. What was wrong with him? This little business arrangement with Kylee was only supposed to be a temporary pause to his social life. Not a complete overhaul of it.

***You tell Mom or Dad about the marriage yet?***

Mason clearly wasn't done with their conversation.

***No, I'll probably tell them tomorrow.***

***Quit putting it off. You need to do it before you get here. For Kylee's sake.***

***Thanks, Dr. Phil. Any other sage advice you want to give?***

***Happy wife, happy life.***

Ryan scratched his head absentmindedly. He did need to tell his parents. And he would—soon. But right now, he had to finish these forecasts. Putting his phone on silent, he turned back to the computer.

Kylee should be back from her run any minute now. Ryan was waiting on her before he ordered any kind of takeout.

His patience was rewarded five minutes later when he heard the front door open and close. He told himself to stay in his chair, not wanting to seem overly eager to have her home. Despite his resolve, he found himself walking into the living room.

"How was the run?" he asked as he leaned against the wall.

Kylee, with her back to him, jumped at his words. "Geez, you scared me!"

Ryan cocked one eyebrow. "Who did you think it was going to be?"

She just waved his comment off. "My run was good. I'm pretty sure a snail could beat me in a foot race, but at least I did it." Then, she sat on the couch and groaned. "My calves are going to be feeling it tomorrow."

“I know you say you don’t hike, but we’ll have to go when we’re at my parents’. They have a bunch of cool trails around their house.” He watched her as she began doing some stretches.

Her forehead to her leg, she said, “Ugh. I don’t think I ever will catch on to your love of hiking and camping. I much prefer a quick run and sleeping in my own bed as opposed to a five-hour hike and sleeping in the dirt.”

“Well, technically, you’d be sleeping in a sleeping bag in a tent, but let’s not get specific,” he said, silently wondering how women were always so much more flexible. “Plus, it didn’t hurt growing up with that being a part of my regular life. My mom’s favorite thing to do was to wake us up for early morning hikes before school. And weekends were always some sort of backpacking or camping trip with my dad.”

She turned so she was facing him. “You haven’t really told me any specifics about your family. I probably need to get some details before we go visit them.”

“I’m sure I’ve told you some things about them, haven’t I?”

Kylee shook her head. “I’ve met your brother once—Mike, was it?”

“Mason.”

“That’s right. Mason. I met him about a year ago when I was helping you with marketing content for those hiking boots.”

Ryan nodded, wishing he could have forgotten all about his hiking boots disaster. It had been his first real business start-up and had ended terribly. The product design itself had actually been great. The problems had begun with his overseas manufacturer. The boots had all arrived in pairs of matching right-foot boots. Not a single left-footed shoe had been produced.

When Ryan tried to get in contact with the manufacturers, they disappeared. Literally. Apparently, Ryan's wasn't the only job that had been botched up by the company, and the men in charge had decided it was time to hightail it out of there.

He had tried to find someone else to produce matching left-foot boots, but by then, he was in over his head. The SKUs he'd been scheduled to deliver were already late, and his financiers had backed out.

"But other than that," Kylee continued, "I don't know details about anyone."

"Okay, if you really want to hear about them all, I'll tell you. But first,"—he held up one finger—"I'm starving. What do you want for dinner? I was thinking Thai food or pizza."

"Mmm, let's do pizza."

"I like the way you think," Ryan responded with a grin. He pulled up the local pizza shop's website on his phone. "What are you feeling like? Pepperoni? Ham? Please don't say spinach."

"You're such a carnivore. I should demand we get a veggie one." She gave him a sly grin.

Ryan tried to resist the impulse to scrunch up his nose.

Kylee finally laughed. "I'm good with whatever. Hopefully, this run cancels out whatever calories you top it with."

Ryan grinned as he typed their order into his phone. He went with ham and pineapple. He knew it was a favorite of hers. The website confirmed his purchase, and he set his phone down on the table. "It will be delivered in about thirty minutes," he announced.

"Perfect." Her response was muffled since her face was currently pressed into her shoes in a butterfly stretch. She stood quickly at his comment, though. "That'll give me just enough time to shower so I don't make your living room smell like a gym locker."

"What? There's nothing better than that stale sweat smell. Reminds me of the good old days of high school P.E."

She just waved him off as she headed toward the bathroom.

Ryan settled himself into one corner of the couch and began scanning through his emails. Sometimes, owning his own business was the best. He could work whenever and wherever he wanted. At the same time, he often had a hard time ever turning it off.

Twenty minutes later, though, he was snapped out of his work trance when Kylee returned wearing a worn pair of jeans and a faded t-shirt. Her hair, still wet, was brushed back over one shoulder. There was absolutely nothing seductive or flirtatious about her appearance. Nothing that hinted she was trying to catch his attention. So why was he having such a hard time taking his eyes off of her?

"So, let's have that family history lesson you were going to give me," she said as she settled onto the opposite side of the couch from him.

"You sure you're interested?" he asked.

"Of course. They're my family now." She said this with a straight face, but he saw a glint of humor in her eyes.

"Okay, you asked for it." Ryan leaned back into the couch, lifting his legs to rest on the coffee table. "So, first, there are my parents: Becky and Rob. My mom is..." He thought for a second. "She's sixty-two, which would make my dad sixty-five. They've been married for thirty-five years now. My mom is one of those quiet and observant people. She's the type that takes care of everybody—like, literally, everybody. If anyone in the neighborhood needs help or is in trouble, she's the first person they come to."

He shrugged. "She's pretty amazing, and I could go on about her forever, but I'll just leave it at that." He paused as he thought about his father. "My dad is actually the opposite. He's the loud, outgoing type. The life of the party. You know he likes you when he starts teasing you. He's also super outdoorsy. I'm pretty sure his first love, besides his family, is hunting and fishing."

Kylee was watching him as he spoke.

He threw his hands behind his head as he thought about who to describe next. "You know my younger brother, Mason. He's twenty-eight now but has the brain of a eighteen-year-old."

"I'm sure your opinion has nothing to do with the fact that he's your younger brother," Kylee cut in with a smile.

"Of course not," he answered with a grin. "Despite it all, I love him, and he's probably one of the nicest guys out there. He likes to act like a tough guy, but he wouldn't hurt a fly.

"Then, there's my little sister, Madison. She's the baby of the family and can get away with murder, but she's pretty sweet, so we're all okay with that. She's twenty-two and graduating with her degree in dietetics this year, which is basically the worst because she's always trying to get the rest of us to eat things like vegetables."

"You're kidding. Vegetables?" She threw her head back and laughed. "It's like she wants you to live a long and healthy life or something."

He eyed Kylee through squinted eyes. "Don't try and convince me you believe in things like fruits and vegetables, too."

She threw a pillow at him.

He caught it in midair and smiled back at her. "Finally," he sighed, getting back on track, "there's my grandma. She moved in with my parents about three years ago when her eyesight got bad. She still insists she can take care of herself, but it's a good arrangement for everyone." He stopped and got lost in his thoughts for a moment. "My grandma is a lady full of spunk. Everyone tells me my personality is similar to hers. We're both a little stubborn and headstrong."

Kylee seemed to be studying him. "You *are* kind of stubborn, but I would say it's been an asset in your life, though, not a detriment."

He didn't know why her thought made him feel so good, but it did. "Thank you. I'm pretty sure there are some who would disagree with you, but I appreciate it all the same."

A tinge of pink played on her cheeks, and Ryan wondered if he'd embarrassed her. But before he could ask, there was a loud knock on the door. Ryan jumped up, grateful for the interruption.

"The pizza must be here," he said.

Sure enough, there was a teenage boy holding a giant, sizzling pizza at the door.

After tipping the kid, Ryan kicked the door closed and brought the box over to the table.

"Oh goodness, that smells so good," Kylee exclaimed as she followed him into the kitchen.

Instead of sitting down next to him, though, she collected plates and cups, which she proceeded to fill with water and ice. At the table, she handed him a cup and a plate before sitting down. Ryan loved how she had managed to integrate herself into his life in such a short period of time. As always, it wasn't an effort to feel comfortable with Kylee. It was just natural.

"So, how's work coming along?" she asked, interrupting his thoughts.

"Oh, it's fine. I've been going through emails from potential vendors. Basically just a lot of back and forths before we really get anywhere." Ryan grabbed a giant piece of pizza, the cheese stringing along as he brought it to his plate.

"I'm assuming things have been picking up the last few months with production starting?" she asked before taking a bite of her own piece.

He nodded, the word *production* causing his first bite to lodge in his throat. Considering his entire first production batch had been a total waste, the knowledge that things were picking up was more nerve-racking than exciting. What if he never managed to produce any viable product? "Yeah, things are picking up. But I try to not become a slave to it all. Being your own boss can be a blessing and a curse."

Kylee set her slice on her plate. "Yeah, I feel the same way sometimes. I try setting up parameters for myself, like no working after seven p.m. or on the weekend, but they never last."

It was nice having that bond in common with Kylee. Lots of times, his friends only saw the benefits of running his own company. They never understood that it came with its set of hardships too. "Well, cheers to the entrepreneurial spirit and being workaholics," Ryan said as he lifted his water in a toast.

"Hear, hear!" Kylee agreed, clicking her glass against his. Her trademark smile seemed filled with extra warmth.

Their discussion turned to more lighthearted topics as they finished up. Finally, Kylee stood and took her dishes into the kitchen, talking as she walked. "Well, I better go get some work done too, I suppose. This fake marriage might pay off my student loans, but I still have other bills." When she faced him, she was grinning.

He tried to smile back, but he was sure it looked strained. Her comment brought him back to reality. This was all fake. It was just to get a cash flow to his business to fix things. So why did their relationship feel so real tonight? "Okay," he said, trying to shake it off. "I'll just be out here, finishing off the rest of this pizza."

"Remind me to go to the store and buy some fruits and vegetables tomorrow," she called back as she headed down the hallway.

He smiled at her retreating back then looked around him. The room suddenly felt so empty now, like the life had been taken from it. He scowled at the pizza in his hand. He had to get past these feelings. This marriage wasn't real. A month from now, Kylee would be back at her place, and they'd go back to their normal relationship.

He wished the thought didn't fill him with so much dismay.

*****

The next morning was quiet. Kylee generally liked to sleep in most mornings, so by the time she'd finally roused herself, Ryan was already gone somewhere.

The knowledge that she was alone eased some of her discomfort of waking up in another person's house. Not bothering to change out of her pajamas, she entered the kitchen and made her way to the fridge. Opening the door, she scanned the contents. Despite Ryan's admonishment that he was going to finish off the pizza, there were still a few leftover slices. She grinned and contemplated eating a cold piece for breakfast. Instead, she reached for a half-empty jug of orange juice—the only thing in the fridge that resembled fresh produce—and poured herself a glass.

She made her way into the living room with the cup, settling deep into the couch. She gazed around at the simply decorated room and sighed. This was nice, she told herself. A quiet reprieve after all the chaos of yesterday.

Despite her claim, after a few minutes of silence, she started getting antsy. Where was Ryan, anyway? Maybe she should call him and see if everything was alright. She shook off the feeling, telling herself she was being ridiculous. She was just used to living with a roommate—a rather loud one, at that—so the quiet was getting to her.

She was ten minutes into an infomercial about the latest and greatest treadmill when the front door opened. Ryan stepped inside, looking much too alert and attractive for this early in the day. Kylee pushed the thought aside and tried to appear like she hadn't been brooding over his absence the last little bit.

When he turned and noticed her, his face opened up into a wide-mouth grin. "You're awake. I thought it'd be at least another hour until I saw you." He kicked the door closed behind him, then set the bag he was carrying on the coffee table in front of her. The smell coming from it hinted at some sort of baked good. Kylee noticed he was wearing a loose t-shirt and some jogging shorts. Apparently, he'd visited the gym already as well as gotten breakfast.

"Usually, I'm up by eight. Although, if I let myself, I could probably sleep until noon every day." She'd given up being ashamed of her love of sleep long ago. Mornings were just not in her blood.

He winked at her before settling onto the couch as well. Kylee tried not to note the fact that, instead of sitting at the far end of the sofa, he situated himself in the middle, only about a foot from her. "I know you're not a morning person, which is why I took the liberty of getting us breakfast." He pulled out two bagels halfway wrapped in wax paper. They were still warm, if the steam coming off them gave any indication. "I went basic: two everything bagels with plain shmear." He handed her one.

"Mmmm," she said as she brought the warm bread to her nose. "You know just the way to my heart, Ryan." She felt her face heat up and tried to cover her gaffe by shoving a huge bite in her mouth. The words were innocent enough. It was a comment she could've made even a week ago without thinking twice. But somehow, now that they were married, she worried that everything she said might carry a hint of innuendo or subtle meaning.

Ryan, luckily, didn't seem to think much of it. He handed her a napkin, indicating at the cream cheese she obviously had smeared across her cheek as he eyed her juice on the table. "Orange juice. That's exactly what this needs."

Kylee took a slow breath as he went into the kitchen, willing herself to relax. Everything was the same as it had been two days ago. Sure, they were married now, but it was all a farce. She just needed to act normal and stop worrying that everything she did was going to hint at her real feelings for him.

Ryan came back, resuming his position on the couch. "You interested in a new treadmill?" he asked.

"Huh?" Kylee had decided to focus her thoughts on eating and had obviously missed something he said. "What do you mean?"

He pointed at the TV screen where a burly man was giving his testimonial about how the TX5000 changed his life.

"Oh! No, I was just— I couldn't find anything else. Here,"—she handed him the remote— "you can choose."

He gave her a grin and took the remote from her, his cool fingertips brushing hers slightly. "Sports are my default, if you're okay with that."

She shrugged, and two minutes later, they were watching highlight recaps on ESPN.

They were silent for a minute—a borderline awkward one. "So," she finally said, unable to deal with the quiet anymore, "tell me more about Hudson's Packs. I know they're super-high-quality backpacking bags made with top-of-the-line material." She saw Ryan wince at this comment. "Er, well, they eventually will be made with top-of-the-line material." She hurried on. "But what else makes them so special?"

Ryan cocked his head at her. "You sure you want to get into this? You know once I start talking about hiking, it's hard to get me to stop." One corner of his mouth turned up.

"I'll tell you if you're starting to bore me," she said, grabbing her juice and wiggling to get more comfortable on the couch.

"That's fair," he agreed. "My bags, as you said, are going to be top-of-the-line backpacking equipment. The base material is made of Cordura fabric…"

Ryan was demonstrating all the parts with his hands now, and Kylee was only catching about every other word. Instead, her mind was fixed on his expression and the excitement sparking in his eyes. Their color seemed to deepen as he talked. She loved how eager he got when it came to his company.

"The rest is made with a silicone-coated, rip-stop nylon. It has a standard internal frame and a customizable pocket configuration..."

As he continued talking, she noticed a light scar hinting under his chin. Where had he gotten that? Was it a childhood accident? Kylee realized that, as much as she knew about Ryan from their friendship, there was still so much about him she had left to learn.

"...then the part that lays against the hiker's back is a mesh lining for better airflow."

He rose from his seat and reached out for Kylee's hand, snapping her back to the conversation.

"Here, stand up. I'll show you."

She suddenly felt herself being pulled to a standing position, just barely managing to set her glass back on the table before it spilled.

He turned her around so his hands were on her back. Kylee had to bite back a laugh at his enthusiasm."So the straps run over your shoulders like this and then lay flat against your shoulders here." His fingers were drawing firm lines down her back.

"Underneath the mesh is a memory foam liner to allow more comfort." He began running his finger horizontal now, getting about halfway across her shoulderblades before the firmness in his hand softened. The pressure suddenly became more of a caress than a demonstration, and Kylee realized Ryan had stopped talking.

"So, does the memory foam go over the—" Kylee turned as she started her question, only to find herself inches from his face. The backpack demonstration flew from her mind as time froze.

His hand was still hanging in the air from where he'd been tracing her back, his eyes fixed motionlessly on hers.

She stared into their darkness, for the first time noticing the glints of gold that framed his irises. They had to have been the warmest shade of brown she'd ever seen. They seemed to be searching her eyes just as intently. When his gaze trailed down to her mouth, the blood started pounding in her head. Was he going to kiss her again? There was no court judge expecting it from them now. It would have been entirely of their own accord this time.

His chin started to tilt toward hers, his lifted hand dropping to trail down her arm. The touch sent a trail of goosebumps through her, and she tilted her face up to meet his.

Then he stepped back abruptly.

"Well! Anyway...you, uh, get the picture. A fancy backpack...perfect for any backpacker's dream." Ryan ran a hand through his dark hair, mussing it slightly. "So, uh...speaking of work, I should probably go finish those financial spreadsheets I was working on yesterday."

He had been slowly backing up during this stuttered speech, putting plenty of distance between them.

"So, I'll probably be working most of today, so if you don't see me, that's where I am." His voice carried a false cheeriness to it. He gave an awkward wave before ducking into his office/temporary bedroom and closing the door.

Kylee stared at the closed door with raised eyebrows.

What just happened?

If someone had told Kylee a week ago that she and Ryan would almost kiss (and not just for show in front of a judge), she would've said they were nuts. But she couldn't deny that it had almost happened.

She wanted to be indifferent to it. Shrug it off as just a weird moment. But she couldn't. She couldn't forget the way Ryan smelled up close. Or the way his hand felt on her arm. Or the heightened emotion she'd seen in his gaze.

What had it all meant? Was Ryan developing feelings for her?

She leaned over and grabbed the remote, mentally shaking her thoughts out.

No. This was exactly what she promised herself she wouldn't do. She wouldn't read into things and hope for something permanent to develop between them.

Mindlessly, she flipped through the channels, once again wondering if this whole thing had been a mistake.

# Chapter 6

Ryan had been doing everything he could to avoid Kylee the last two days. In the most inconspicuous way possible, of course. He hoped she hadn't noticed the fact that he had to "run errands" or "jump on a phone call" whenever she was around.

He was sure his unsteady emotions were simply a result of the strange environment he and Kylee had been thrown into. The fact that being around her set his nerves on fire, or that he couldn't help noticing how good she looked in her jeans, or loving the subtle floral scent that seemed to always surround her was obviously just a natural reaction to things. He wasn't actually developing any feelings for Kylee. His mind was just so confused by the knowledge that he was now married to her that it didn't know what to think.

For example, under normal circumstances, there was no way he would've almost kissed her in his living room like he had that first morning. It wasn't until he was tracing the backpack straps over her shoulders that he realized how intimate the gesture was, how close they were standing. Then, when she'd spun around, the only thing he'd been able to think about was how soft her lips had been the last time they'd kissed.

He shook his head and unbuckled his seatbelt. He had just pulled up to the restaurant where he was meeting his accountant for lunch. They were going to run through some numbers together. Ryan looked at the clock; he had a few minutes to spare.

Pulling out his phone, he decided to call his parents. He'd been putting off telling them about his hasty marriage, but it was probably time to spill the beans. He and Kylee were driving down to visit tomorrow, after all.

His mom answered on the third ring, her cheery voice putting his nerves to rest.

"Hello?"

"Hey, Mom, it's your favorite child."

Without missing a beat, his mom cried out, "Madison, so good to hear from you."

"Ha ha, nice try, Mom." Ryan grinned despite the fact that she couldn't see him. "How are things going at home?"

"Oh, everything's good, *Ryan*. Dad's out fixing something in the shed right now. I'm whipping up a batch of cookies for the Davidsons. Poor Bill fell and broke his leg last week..."

Ryan listened as his mom gave him an update on the neighbors. They lived in a more rural area, meaning everyone knew everything about everyone.

"Anyway, enough about the neighborhood," she finally said. "Tell me about you. What's new? Don't tell me you're trying to back out of this weekend."

Dismay filled her voice, so Ryan was quick to reassure her. "Don't worry, Mom, I'm still coming. Although, this weekend is the reason I'm calling. I have some news to share with you all."

"News?"

Her curiosity was so evident that Ryan wished he had something good to tell her. Instead, he was about to fill her head with a lie. "Yes, pretty, uh, exciting news, really." He took a deep breath. "I got married last week."

There was silence on the other end.

"Mom?" He hoped his news hadn't shocked her into a heart attack or something. "Mom? You still there?"

"I'm—yes, I'm still here. But did you just say you got *married* last week?"

He laughed nervously, wanting to be anywhere other than sitting on the phone feeding his mom lies. "Yep. I sealed the deal. Tied the knot."

"But...to who? I didn't even know you were dating anyone."

"Well, we've kept it somewhat under wraps. I—we, that is—wanted to keep things just between the two of us, you know?" The silence on the other end told him he wasn't selling his story very well. He tried to remember the script he'd practiced. "Kylee, my wife, and I have actually been work acquaintances for a few years now. She is a freelance designer and has worked on several projects for me over the years..." He let his words trail off, not exactly sure how much detail to give. He and Kylee hadn't really discussed what story they were going to tell his family about their past. He figured he had better wait and talk with her before saying too much.

"Anyway, I'm bringing her this weekend, so I just wanted to give you guys the heads up." He spoke quickly, hoping to wrap things up.

"Wait. So, her name is Kylee? How long have you guys worked together? Where's she from? I have so many questions, Ryan! How could you not tell us?!" Her voice held more shock than dismay, for which he was glad. Under normal circumstances, he never would have considered marrying someone without involving his family in the event.

"I know, there's so much to tell. We'll give you all the details when we see you all this weekend."

"Well...are you sure...okay, I guess this weekend will be fine. But Ryan…" She paused, the stillness feeling heavy even across the phone. "Tell me this, at least. Are you happy?"

The question took him aback. That wasn't what he was expecting. "Yes, Mom, I'm very happy."

"Well then, I guess that's all that matters."

After they hung up, he pondered his answer. He *was* happy. The thought surprised him. He expected to feel nerves—even burdened—by this marriage, but happy? Yes, he couldn't deny the fact that coming home, knowing Kylee would be there, put a smile on his face. Why was he working so hard to avoid her, anyway? As his mom had exposed, being with Kylee made him happy.

The question was, where did that leave him when this was all over?

*****

Kylee twisted the ring on her third finger, mid-morning on Tuesday.

She was once again in her favorite chair, in her favorite coffee shop, working. Or at least that was what she was supposed to be doing. She needed to finish freshening up a local real estate company's website before she left this weekend.

But no matter how hard she tried to focus, her thoughts kept going back to the last few days with Ryan.

She'd purposely worked at local coffee shops yesterday and today to get out of his condo. She was afraid that the more time she spent with him, the more her little crush (as Elena liked to call it) would grow.

Her phone started vibrating in her bag, so she reached down to get it. It was Elena calling. She'd called on Sunday, but Kylee had been in Ryan's condo, so she hadn't spoken as openly as she normally would have. She sent Elena to voicemail and quickly typed out a text.

***Let me call you back in 5.***

She packed up her bag, stowing her laptop safely in the side pocket and her notepad in the main section. Outside, she found an empty park bench and dialed Elena's phone number.

Her roommate answered on the first ring. "There's my *amiga*. How's the little homemaker?"

"You are ridiculous," Kylee replied.

"Where are you?"

"In a shopping center," she answered. "I was working when you first called."

"Oh, good, so you're free to talk. Spill it, sister."

Kylee fiddled with the zipper on her bag. "We just talked two days ago. What else do you want to know?"

"Everything."

Taking a deep breath, she began giving Elena a more in-depth summary of the last three days. There actually wasn't much to tell. Married life really wasn't that exciting, probably because she was doing her best to interact with Ryan as little as possible. Elena was a rapt audience, all the same.

"So," she said when Kylee was done, "what kind of vibes are you getting from him?"

"Vibes?"

"Yes, *chica*! Has he tried to make any moves on you? I can tell there must have been some sparks from that kiss you described—"

"He was obligated to kiss me," Kylee said over her. "The judge basically ordered him to."

"—so I wouldn't be surprised if he tried it again soon," Elena finished, totally ignoring her comment.

"To answer you, no. Other than carrying me across the threshold, we've barely had any contact." She didn't mention the tension-filled backpack demonstration from a couple nights ago. After that little moment, Ryan also seemed to be doing all he could to avoid spending time with her.

"He carried you across the threshold? Now, that's what I'm talking about! What are you doing, leaving details like that out?"

"It was no big deal, Elena. He was just trying to be funny."

"What it is, is evidence that he has some feelings for you. Why else would he go through the effort? He could've very easily said, 'Welcome to my house, here's your room, try not to use all the hot water,' and left it at that." Elena's tone had changed to a deep one that Kylee assumed was supposed to be Ryan's.

"Have you ever considered voice impersonation?" Kylee asked. "You're actually pretty good."

"Oh, stop trying to change the subject. I'm just saying you can't stick your head in the sand and ignore all the clues going on around you. I can feel these romance vibes underfoot, even if you can't."

Kylee sucked in a deep breath and watched several people walk in and out of the coffee shop. It took effort, but she shoved her jealousy down. Those people didn't have to contend with fake marriages and all-too-real feelings for one of their best friends. She'd have loved to be living a more simple life, but this was what she'd signed up for.

"Nothing is going to happen. Ryan doesn't feel that way about me and never will, and it's something I am perfectly aware of. But thank you for your concern."

"All I know is that I have a bad feeling about this. I think you guys just need to have an honest discussion about your feelings. Put everything on the table and clear the air."

"As sound as your advice is," Kylee said, scratching at the bench's peeling paint with her nail, "I am not going to place my heart out in the open to possibly get trodden upon, thank you very much."

Elena's suggestion was probably the most mature thing to do. The tension slowly building between Kylee and Ryan was definitely confusing. But Kylee knew she could never do it.

After their conversation ended, Kylee stayed on the bench for another minute, thinking about her life. Despite Elena's advice, she concluded that the best thing to do was to guard her emotions. Ryan's meaningless flirting was finding ways to wriggle into her heart, something that would just throw another wrench into their already-complicated situation.

Sighing, she slowly stood, her stomach rumbling at the movement. She had another thirty minutes before her shift at the library, so she decided to go back to the coffee shop and grab something to eat.

A growling stomach she could fix. Her aching heart was something else.

*****

She walked into an empty condo that evening. She didn't know where Ryan was. They hadn't gotten to the point where they briefed each other on their schedules every morning.

After wandering into the kitchen, she put away the bag of groceries she bought on her way home. She stowed her somewhat excessive number of frozen meals in the freezer. That buy-one-get-one-free deal had been hard to pass up. Maybe after this whole marriage arrangement was over and her school debts were gone, she'd be able to stop penny pinching so much.

Sighing, she tossed a meal into the microwave. Then, she grabbed a glass out of the cupboard and filled it with water, noticing a sticky note on the counter as she did it.

*Hey, I have a meeting with a prospective buyer this evening. I'll probably be home around 8. -Ryan*

The note gave her a surprising wave of pleasure. The fact that he'd thought enough to tell her where he was going to be made her feel special.

She grabbed the note, studying his writing. She'd seen it before, obviously. It was a combination of bold and confident strokes, similar to Ryan himself. The thought made the wave of pleasure dissipate.

Who was she kidding? He hadn't done anything special or extraordinary for her. He just didn't want her to worry about him for dinner. He was being polite.

Kylee crumpled the note and tossed it into the trash.

The microwave dinged, and she took her dinner out of it. Unfortunately, she forgot to heed the warning to let it cool for two minutes. She spent the next few minutes dancing around the kitchen, blowing on the tips of her burnt fingers.

After creating a makeshift ice pack with a Ziploc bag and some ice cubes, she grabbed the premade dinner and made her way to her bedroom to pack. She needed to keep a hold of her emotions and thoughts. She had to be on her A-game.

Because tomorrow, she was meeting her in-laws.

# Chapter 7

They were ten minutes into their drive, and Ryan had already run out of casual things to talk about. But his mind was filled with questions that just seemed too intimate to ask.

They'd covered the weather, work, and traffic, and now, they were at a standstill. He did the only thing he could think of. He turned on the radio.

"What do you want to listen to?"

Kylee shrugged, her gold earrings bouncing haphazardly at the motion. Her dark, fitted skirt went well with the white, flowy top she was wearing. She had also done something different with her hair so it hung in loose waves that seemed to float down her back. She, apparently, had taken extra effort with her appearance this morning.

He should have told her not to worry about it. His family was as casual and easygoing as anyone could get. He doubted he'd ever seen his mom wear a stitch of makeup in her life, and his dad's idea of dressing up was putting on a clean shirt.

But he couldn't help enjoying the view from his seat. Not that she needed all the extra fluff to look good. She was one of those girls who was just beautiful naturally.

"How about you?" Kylee's comment snapped him out of his thoughts.

"How about me what?"

"Anything you want to listen to?"

"Oh, I'm an oldies fan." He gave her a wink. "I'm basically a fifty-year-old at heart."

She smiled and began messing with the radio dial herself.

A song came on that Ryan was sure she wouldn't know, but she stopped at it. When the chorus started and she began singing right along with it, he looked at her with wide eyes.

"You know this song?"

"'All Right Now' by Free? One of the greatest hits in the early seventies." She gave him a smug look. "I might have a little grandpa in me, too."

Sparks of pleasure lit up in Ryan. Obviously, from finding another music lover, he told himself. Definitely not from the way Kylee's eyes sparkled when she smiled at him.

They spent the next half hour listening to oldies music and discussing some of their favorites. Kylee was a soul fan, but Ryan leaned more toward the beginning of the rock-and-roll era.

"There is, literally, not a single person on the Earth who doesn't love the song 'Ain't No Mountain High Enough,'" Kylee said with a defiant hand wave.

"That's possible, but Led Zeppelin's 'Stairway to Heaven' literally changed music as we know it."

Kylee shook her head. "Are you serious? That song puts me to sleep faster than a lullaby."

"How dare you. Take it back."

She grinned at him. "The real question is, how did I not know this about you?"

"Know what?"

"Your love for the oldies. How have we never discussed it before?"

Ryan raised his eyebrows. "I don't know. Apparently, there are still some things about each other we need to discover." What else about Kylee did *he* not know yet?

Kylee leaned back into her seat, a content smile playing at the edges of her mouth. "All right, enough music talk. Let's talk about something serious. We need to go over what our stories are going to be this weekend. We need to make sure I'm not telling people we met at a friend's birthday party and you're telling people we met on a blind date."

"First off, both those stories are totally boring," Ryan responded. "If I was going to make something up, it would be pretty cool. Like, we met while skydiving in the

Bahamas. Both of us were midair when our eyes locked across the wide expanse, and we knew, at that moment, if we were going to die, we'd die together. Our hands locked as we vowed—"

"Okay, make sure you never become a screenwriter," Kylee cut in, placing a hand on his shoulder.

The pressure from her fingers sent a flush of warmth through Ryan, and for a moment, he struggled to focus on driving.

"Fine, no skydiving stories," he responded, getting ahold of himself. "I think we should just stick with the truth—or at least as close to the truth as possible. We met a couple years ago when you did a design for me while I cut my entrepreneurial teeth on the worst product fail ever."

"C'mon," she said. "It wasn't that bad."

"Kylee. I made *no* money on those hiking boots. None. As a matter of fact, I was painfully in the red. All my investors lost everything on that one." Ryan still cringed when he thought about his hiking boots debacle.

He blew out a breath and tried to blot the memory from his mind. "Anyway, you were my designer for the project, and we worked on and off on that for several months."

Kylee picked it up from there. "One thing led to another, and the next thing you knew, you had asked me out on a date. That lunch date led to another."

"Then, the next thing *you* knew," Ryan cut in, a sly smile forming on his lips, "you had the hots for me and couldn't keep your hands to yourself—"

"Hey!" Kylee interjected.

"Okay," he said, grinning. "I had the hots for you. I begged you to go out with me again. I fought off all your other suitors and won the hand of the fair maiden."

"I feel like we're not addressing the issue here," Kylee said, lifting an eyebrow.

"Fine, fine. Let's get serious." He steered with one hand while he counted off with his other. "First, we met when you were doing design work for me. Second, we started officially dating when I asked you out on a date."

"What kind of date did we go on?"

He arched an eyebrow. "I don't know. Does it matter?"

"Yes, first dates matter!" she exclaimed, her eyes wide as she faced him. "*Someone* is going to ask what we did."

"Fine." He thought it over as he made a left turn. "We walked around the farmer's market near the library. I ended up buying you a scarf you were admiring, and we ate the best ice cream we'd ever had. Afterwards, we got pizza somewhere." Then, he turned to look at her with lifted eyebrows.

"I like it. Good idea."

Ryan's mouth raised at one corner. "So, we went out on our first date, one thing led to another, and we were seriously dating. Next thing we knew, we'd fallen madly in love—"

"Where did you first say 'I love you' to me?"

"No one's going to ask that!"

"Probably not, but it'd be good to have a few stories to beef up our act."

Ryan had to give it to her. She had a point. "Alright, you come up with this one."

She was silent a moment. "We went on a bike ride around the reservoir around sunset. Then, on that bridge near the back side, you told me you loved me."

"Not too shabby yourself," he said, giving her the side eye.

"I missed my calling as a romance author," Kylee replied, sighing dramatically.

"So I said 'I love you.' Of course, you returned the sentiment immediately—"

Kylee coughed loudly.

"—and now we need an engagement story," Ryan said, ignoring her jab.

She shrugged. "The ball's in your court. How would you propose to me in real life?"

Suddenly, Ryan had an image flash through his mind of him bending down on one knee in front of Kylee. The visual was clear as day. The surreal part was that the thought didn't scare him.

"Ryan?"

"Uh, what?" he asked, noticing his knuckles turning white on the steering wheel. He tried to relax. "Oh yeah, how would I propose to you?" He ran one hand through his hair. "Let's see. I'd probably do it somewhere private. I never could get behind guys who propose in the middle of a crowd or something. Let's say we went for a hike as the sun was rising..."

"Ugh, I hate early mornings," Kylee cut in.

"But remember, you're deeply in love with me, so you'll hike with me anywhere, anytime," Ryan continued without missing a beat. "And as we reached the viewpoint, I knelt down on one knee and proposed with the most beautiful diamond solitaire you'd ever seen."

She twisted the ring on her finger. "Please tell me this isn't real, is it?" she asked, uncertainty in her tone.

Ryan cringed slightly as he glanced at her. "No. It's cubic zirconia."

After a moment of silence, she reached over and patted his arm. "It's okay, dear," she said, and he could've sworn she was biting her cheek. "I'm sure one day we'll be able to afford the real thing."

He snorted. "Alright, so we got most of our storylines figured out, and I think we know enough about each other to answer personal questions."

"Do we?" She twisted in her seat to face him again. "What's my favorite color?"

"Purple."

"What's my coffee order?"

"You don't drink coffee."

"What's my shoe size?"

"Uh...seven?"

"Close," Kylee said with a grin. "Seven and a half, but I'm impressed."

"So, like I said, I think we know enough about each other." He tapped his thumbs on the steering wheel, trying not to let his smugness show. "I think the one thing we need to work on is our physicality."

"Our what?"

A flush slowly rode up Ryan's neck. "Our lovey-doveyness. Our PDA. We're supposed to be newlyweds. I think people are going to notice if we never come near each other."

Kylee bit her lip.

"Look, I don't want to put you in any uncomfortable positions. I just know my family is going to think it's weird if we don't show some affection for each other while we're there. Isn't our main reason for eloping because we couldn't stand to be apart another day?"

"I guess. It just makes us sound so...juvenile." She shrugged. "But you're right. I don't know what other reason we could use."

"That we married so I could get access to my trust fund and I could save my failing business? The second business I've almost lost in the last three years."

"Well, I wouldn't put it that bluntly, but yes." With Kylee beaming at him, things felt a little more lighthearted.

"All right, wifey." Ryan glanced at his watch. "About another ten minutes before you meet your new in-laws."

*****

Kylee had been mentally chanting, "Stay calm, stay calm," for the last five minutes. She wanted to appear composed when she met Ryan's family, but the vise grip she had on the edges of her seat weren't boding well for her.

When Ryan had pulled off the highway, they went a half mile farther before turning down a long driveway. In front of them laid a beautiful ranch-style home that was well kept but still had a rustic vibe to it.

There were two cars and two trucks parked in the long driveway. Ryan pulled his sedan up behind them all and turned the engine off.

He turned to Kylee as he took his seatbelt off. "Are you ready?"

She swallowed, not sure why she had gotten herself into this mess in the first place. "I guess I'm as ready as I'll ever be," she said and unclicked her own seatbelt.

He reached over and patted her shoulder. "I know I'm asking a ton of you right now, Kylee. But remember, this is my family. Just the fact that you were willing to marry what my parents have considered their hopeless son,"—she could see him trying not to laugh—"is enough to make them love you."

"You *are* kind of hopeless," she responded, trying to catch hold of his light mood. She swallowed again. "How long have they known about us being married?"

He bit his cheek. "I, uh, told them yesterday."

"Yesterday! You didn't tell them we got married until yesterday?" Kylee felt the color drain from her face.

"Time got away from me." Ryan's arm flew back at his side. "I'm sorry."

She took a deep breath as she rolled her shoulders back. "All right. It's fine. Let's go pretend to be madly in love with each other."

He grinned. "I will probably owe you forever."

She felt a little spark of warmth at his comment. *Forever?*

As they got out of the car, Ryan reached for her hand. She gave it to him, knowing they had to start playing up the "touchy feely" part of their relationship as Ryan named it. The way his fingers wrapped around her hand, though, like a strong, yet somehow gentle glove, sent goosebumps up her arm that she had no problem faking. When they reached the door, Ryan didn't knock. Instead, he just turned the knob and pushed it open.

"Hello?" he called out in the entryway. "Anyone home?"

"Ryan!" a soft voice called from another room, and a second later, a woman who looked to be in her late sixties came into view. This must've been Ryan's mom.

She didn't actually look much like Ryan. She had fair skin and hair in comparison to his dark coloring, and her features were much more delicate. However, her eyes lit up like his, and she had the same expressive mouth.

Ryan dropped Kylee's hand as his mom pulled him in for a tight hug, murmuring what sounded like, "Welcome home." Then, she turned to Kylee.

Kylee's heart pounded, and she tried to discreetly wipe her now sweaty palms on the back of her skirt. "Hello, Mrs. Hudson. I'm so glad to finally meet you."

"Oh, call me Becky!" Ryan's mom pulled Kylee into a hug too, a warm scent of something cinnamony enveloping her.

It was one of those hugs she didn't want to let go of. It felt safe. Her mom had always been very loving, however, she never gave off the protective feeling Ryan's mom seemed to own.

"Here, let me look at you," his mom said as she stepped back. She held Kylee at arm's length and studied her. "You're every bit as pretty as Mason said you were," she said with a smile. "But more importantly, you appear to have a good soul. Considering you managed to convince Ryan into matrimony, I would expect nothing less."

"All right, all right, Mom. Enough of that. You don't want to scare Kylee off too soon, or she'll never come back." He put his arm on Kylee's shoulder and steered her toward the back of the house.

His mom swatted his comment away. "Dad's in the family room, and I'm just pulling a batch of cinnamon rolls out of the oven."

Cinnamon rolls? Kylee couldn't remember the last time she'd had a homemade cinnamon roll. Probably never, unless she counted the frozen ones that came in a can. Her mom hadn't been much of a baker when she'd been growing up.

As they walked deeper into the home, Kylee peered around. The inside of the house was decorated more for functionality than looks. The floors were distressed wood—but the real kind of distressing that came from years of use. The main living area was an open room that connected the kitchen, the dining space, and the family room. The furniture was all large, oversized pieces built for comfort. The walls were mostly filled with family pictures with a few landscapes here and there.

As she entered the room, Kylee noticed a man lounging on a sectional couch, watching a basketball game on TV.

One glance at the man told her he was Ryan's father. This man was the mirror image of him. Maybe with a few extra wrinkles.

"Ryan," his loud, booming voice filled the space. He came forward, giving Ryan a hug, complete with a few pounds on the back.

When he turned to Kylee, she held out her own hand a little cautiously. She hoped she wouldn't receive the same bone-crushing welcome Ryan had gotten.

"And you must be Kylee." He ignored her outstretched hand and enveloped her in a hug.

As wonderful as Ryan's mom's hug had been, his dad's was almost better. It was literally like being swaddled in a giant blanket.

"So glad you guys could make it. How was the drive?" Ryan's dad asked when she stepped back. His voice had lowered a few decibels, but it still filled the room.

"It was good. No traffic or anything," Ryan replied.

"And how is married life treating you?" he asked, directing his comment to Kylee.

"Uh, it's good," Kylee stuttered. She hadn't thought she would be questioned so soon. Rebounding quickly, she added, "It really is great, Mr. Hudson. Ryan is the best thing that's ever happened to me." She wrapped her arm around Ryan's waist and glanced up at him in what she hoped was an adoring look.

His dad looked back and forth between them, a slight grin on his face. "No Mr. Hudsons around here; I'm just Rob to you. Well, I'm happy for you. And I'm even more happy you decided to get married without telling us so your mom couldn't force me to put on a tux."

"Oh, when's the last time I've ever been able to make you do anything you didn't want to?" Ryan's mom asked, waving a hand towel at him. Turning to Ryan and Kylee, she said, "I can't lie. I'm a little disappointed that I didn't get to see my firstborn say his wedding vows to the love of his life." She looked pointedly at Ryan during this little speech. "But I guess it doesn't really matter in the long run. As long as you two have found each other and are happy, I'm happy."

Kylee was glad the comment was directed toward Ryan, because the guilt was already getting to her.

Ryan shrugged and shuffled his feet for a second before changing the subject. "So, where is everybody else? Where are Gram and Mason? And where's Madison?"

"Oh, Grandma's taking a nap. Mason had to go into town for something. And Madison is driving in this morning, too."

As she was saying this, a voice spoke out behind them.

"Is that you making all this racket, Ryan?"

Kylee glanced over her shoulder at the older woman entering the room. She was wearing a soft pair of jeans and a loose knitted sweater. Though she was a slight little thing, her voice was strong, and her eyes were sharp.

"Grandma," Ryan called out, walking toward her. "I'm so happy to see you."

"Don't try and sweet-talk me, boy. I want to be introduced to this girl of yours." Despite her comment, she accepted the hug Ryan gave her. Her eyes, however, remained locked on Kylee.

Ryan reached back and took Kylee's hand, bringing her forward. "Grandma, this is Kylee. Kylee, this is my grandma."

His grandma reached forward and enclosed one of Kylee's hands in both of hers. The sharpness in her gaze stayed as she studied Kylee. Kylee wasn't sure if she should have spoken first or remained silent. Somehow, interrupting his grandma's perusal seemed rude.

Finally, the moment was broken. "Kylee, I'm happy to meet you. We have been trying to get this boy to settle down for years, and I'd just about given up hope until he called yesterday. Welcome to the family." Despite her friendly words, Kylee still wasn't convinced of their reliability. She was pretty sure his grandma still had some reservations about the marriage, if the firm line her mouth was pressed in gave any hint.

"Thank you. I'm so happy to be here, too. Ryan has spoken nonstop about you all." What was one more white lie compared to everything else she'd been doing? She stepped an inch closer to Ryan, his presence giving her a sense of security.

They spent the next few minutes chatting and gathering around the kitchen island as Ryan's mom pulled the warm cinnamon rolls off the pan. Despite his grandma's reaction, Kylee could barely believe the immediate warmth and acceptance she'd received from Ryan's parents. For some reason, she had been expecting them to be more disapproving and suspicious.

Her nerves had almost disappeared when a voice called out from the front door. "I sure hope you saved me a cinnamon roll."

Kylee turned to see a beautiful girl walk into the kitchen.

"Madison!" Rob's deep voice boomed. Kylee was beginning to learn that this was his normal volume level.

Madison dropped the bag that had been slung over her shoulder and gave her dad a big hug. In turn, she gave her mom and grandma hugs as well. Only then did she face Ryan and Kylee.

"Ryan, I hear you have some big news to tell me," she said as she gave him a hug, one that seemed rather stilted to Kylee.

"Yep. You've complained your whole life that you never had a sister, so I got you one." He winked as he turned to Kylee. "Kylee, this is my little sister, Madison. Madison,"—he stared at Kylee for a split second—"this is my *wife*, Kylee."

Kylee reached her arms out, planning to go in for a hug since it appeared that it was this family's standard greeting. But she was abruptly stopped when Madison stuck out her hand for a formal handshake.

"Pleasure to meet you, Kylee. It's a pity none of us were able to make it to your wedding." She raised her eyebrows. "It seemed to happen rather quickly. Ryan never mentioned he was dating anyone when we last spoke a couple weeks ago."

Kylee didn't know how to respond to the underhanded accusation. It was clear the situation had rubbed Madison the wrong way. Not that Kylee faulted her for it, but it did bring all the nerves right back to the surface. Would Madison cause them trouble convincing everyone?

Luckily, Ryan cut in. "Sorry, sis. I knew you'd spill the beans to everyone else if I told you about her." He slung his arm around Kylee and pulled her close. "I just wanted to keep her to myself for a little bit." He finished off his speech with a kiss on top of Kylee's head.

Kylee was pretty sure her stiff face betrayed his story.

"Hmm," was all Madison responded with.

Probably noticing the tension in the air, Ryan's mom interrupted their chat before Madison could speculate further.

"Why don't I show you two to your room? I put you in the green room at the far end of the house."

Kylee raised her eyes at Ryan. *The green room?*

Ryan immediately started laughing. "My mother's a little pretentious and likes to pretend our home is similar to the White House. We have themed, colored rooms and everything."

"Oh hush," said his mother. "I do not. It's just the easiest way to identify the different rooms in this house." She turned and began speaking to Kylee. "This place used to be a working ranch, so the house actually has seven bedrooms. They were originally used to accommodate all the ranch hands, once upon a time." She eyed Ryan. "So, instead of labeling the rooms with a number, I usually refer to them by the color they're painted. The room you'll be staying in has walls that have been painted a mint-green color. Hence the name."

"That sounds perfectly logical. I would probably do the same thing," Kylee responded.

Stopping in her tracks, Ryan's mom gave him a pointed look. "I like her already."

When they started walking again, Ryan took Kylee's hand and squeezed. When she glanced at his face, he mouthed a silent "thank you" followed by a smile. She wasn't sure what exactly he was referring to. Maybe he thought she had played her opening scene well out there with his family. Whatever his reasons, she couldn't help liking the feeling of his hand around hers or the appreciative look in his eye.

Only when Becky stopped at the last door in the hall did the implications of their situation suddenly hit her. Ryan's mom was showing them to *their* room. *One* room. As in, a single room a married couple would obviously share. With about a 99% probability of only having one bed.

She glanced over her shoulder at Ryan, hoping to see the wheels of his mind turning, searching for a solution. He just gave her an innocent look in return. Well, this was great. How in the world were they going to navigate this?

Kylee stepped into the room. As expected, the room was painted a pale mint green, a shade that blended seamlessly with the white accents in the room, like the dresser, the side tables…

And the *one* bed.

"This room is lovely!" was her quick response. In her head, though, alarms were going off.

"Thank you. I hope you'll be comfortable here. There's a stack of clean towels in the bathroom, which is the next door over," Becky said, indicating with her arm.

"Mom, I may not have grown up in this house, but I've stayed here at least a hundred times. I can show Kylee around," Ryan responded in a dry tone. He turned to Kylee. "My parents moved into this house right as I left for college. As such, I've never had a designated room here. You could say I'm somewhat of a black sheep."

"You are ridiculous," his mom said as she rolled her eyes. "I'll let you two get situated. Dinner will be in about an hour." She paused at the door. "Dinner will just be us and Grandma, but we're having most of the family over for dessert tonight. I think tomorrow we're going to do actual dinner with everyone."

"*Everyone*?" Ryan asked, cringing slightly.

His mother bit her cheek, and Kylee could've sworn she was holding back a smile. "Yes. Prepare yourselves."

Then she was gone, and it was just the two of them.

Ryan closed the door softly then turned to look at Kylee.

"So," she said, sitting down on the bed. "What are we going to do about this sleeping situation?"

*****

A half an hour later, Kylee followed Ryan back to the main room, where the smell of roasting meat had managed to draw everyone. Even Mason had shown up, which made her feel a little better. Someone who knew about their ruse was around. He would hopefully be an ally.

"Ryan," Mason cried from the couch, chucking a pillow at him as he walked into the room. "Have you gained a few pounds the last week or so? You're looking a little fuller around the waist." He motioned with his hands around his torso.

"No, dude. You're obviously just referring to my six-pack. After dinner, I can show you what a push-up is and maybe you can get a few muscles of your own."

Despite their teasing, they walked toward each other and embraced in a tight hug. Ryan did, of course, have to follow up the hug by mussing Mason's hair. Kylee loved the easy relationship they had.

"Kylee," Mason called out, moving toward her with open arms.

Happy to see a somewhat-familiar face, Kylee fell into the embrace with a grateful sigh. "It's good to see you again, Mason."

"How's my brother treating you? Do I need to rough him up a bit or anything?"

Kylee laughed, comforted by the total acceptance she seemed to be getting from Ryan's family. Well, almost total. Madison was still staring her down from the corner of the room.

"He hasn't acted up yet," Kylee responded, "but I'll let you know if things change."

Mason simply nodded.

"You all better get in here while the food is hot." Ryan's mom's voice floated toward them, a stark contrast to the loudness of all the other members of her family.

As commanded, they all made their way to the dining room table. The array of homestyle food was laid out in several bowls and platters: mashed potatoes, biscuits, green beans, and what looked to be a roast. Kylee couldn't remember the last time she'd eaten such a hearty meal.

Ryan's dad said a quick blessing on the food, and they all dug in.

Every dish was passed around at least twice, and Kylee made sure to grab a serving of everything each time.

She had just taken a bite of roast beef, which was the most melt-in-your-mouth thing she'd ever tasted, when the interrogation began.

"So," Ryan's grandma began as she broke apart a biscuit, "how did you two actually meet?"

Kylee gave Ryan a smile. "Why don't you tell the story, hon?"

He told their history of working together, elaborating on a few parts for his family's benefit.

Kylee nodded and smiled at all the right places, even going so far as to lovingly massage his shoulder at one point. She was impressing herself with her acting skills. Although, it didn't take much effort. She would've been perfectly happy to have been sitting there, telling Ryan's family how they'd met and dated in real life, not just in their made-up life.

The thought made her drop her arm. She picked up her fork and began picking at the food that didn't look quite as appetizing as it had a minute ago.

This wouldn't ever be real life.

"So was it love at first sight?" Madison asked, and Kylee was sure she'd heard sarcasm in her question.

Ryan turned to Kylee with raised eyebrows.

"Um, not exactly love at first sight." Kylee played with her mashed potatoes as she spoke. "I think things started growing between us almost without our knowing it. One minute, we were simply business associates who got together occasionally, and the next thing we knew, we were hanging out all the time. It was like we began to depend on each other without realizing or planning on it."

When she looked up from her plate, she found Ryan staring at her intently, a look in his eyes she couldn't define.

"What was it that attracted you to our Ryan?" his dad asked next, interrupting the momentary silence.

"Basically, when she found out I wasn't available, she had to settle for my look-alike older brother," Mason interjected, an innocent expression on his face.

Kylee appreciated his attempt at humor. These questions were getting a little personal for her. At the same time, though, being honest about her attraction to Ryan would probably just add fuel to their story. Ryan would just assume she was playing along as well.

"As Mason said, Ryan's very good-looking." Kylee tried to fight the flush that filled her cheeks. "I'm pretty sure everywhere we go he has all the girls' eyes on him. But obviously, it was more than that. Ryan is one of those people who truly has a good heart. And despite the tough exterior he puts off sometimes—"

Ryan cleared his throat loudly at this.

"—he's one of the kindest people I've ever met." She patted his leg and grinned.

His dad smiled. "I think we all have to agree with you on that one."

"And the first thing that attracted me to Kylee, besides how beautiful she is," Ryan cut in, "is how genuine and real she is. I've never once felt like she was trying to put on a show or pretend to be someone she isn't." He put his arm around her shoulders. "Her goodness is one hundred percent from the heart."

He smiled, and Kylee's actual heart stopped beating for a few seconds. Was that how he truly felt about her? Did he think she was *beautiful*? Did he think she was such a genuine person?

Or was it all just a part of his marriage act?

The interrogation ended for a little bit after that. The topics switched between Madison's schooling and Mason's work. Kylee made a comment here and there, but for the most part, she just listened. She wasn't sure she trusted her emotions at this point.

Ryan's family clearly loved each other. There was constant teasing going on, but the undertones of it all were fun.

His grandma surprised Kylee by being in the heart of it all. She had no problem calling people out or getting in on the banter.

"Mason, you'd better rethink your dating strategy if you ever plan to have any posterity. Girls don't like men who can't commit." She narrowed her eyes at him.

"You mean, you don't think his 'date a different girl every night' method is working?" Ryan responded.

"Whoa, whoa. You guys are blowing things way out of proportion." Mason speared a piece of meat on his fork and brandished it like a weapon. "First off, my strategy is to date a different girl every *week*, not night. I have some class."

"Oh Mason," his mom responded amidst a chorus of laughter from the rest of the table.

"And it's only because I haven't found the right one yet. As soon as I find my 'Kylee' I'll settle down right away like these two lovebirds."

Everyone turned to look at the two lovebirds at this comment. But they were saved from being back in the limelight by his mother's exclamation.

"Goodness! It's already past six thirty. Everyone will be here in about ten minutes." She stood and began stacking plates. "Everyone help clear the table, please. Except you, of course, Mom. You just sit tight." She took Grandma's plate from her.

"Psh, you treat me like I'm on my deathbed," Ryan's grandma said as she pushed her chair back. "I'm just as capable of carrying in a plate or bowl as the rest of you." She eyed Mason, who was struggling to carry in the platter of leftover roast beef. "Probably more capable than some," she muttered just loud enough for Kylee to hear.

Kylee bit back a smile as she stacked several cups on her plate.

Ryan watched her as he held his single plate and cup. "Are you sure you're not going to drop that?"

Kylee followed his gaze to her plate and then smiled. "C'mon, Ryan. You know I paid my way through college serving as a bus girl. Those are skills that never leave." She looked at the plate in her hands. "This is nothing."

Ryan laughed and followed her into the kitchen. "I forgot about that. Apparently, I hit the jackpot with you."

"Clearly," she responded, once again wondering how sincere his compliment was. She wasn't sure if she was going to make it through this entire weekend with all the mental battles she'd already had with herself.

*****

As Ryan's mother had predicted, there was a loud knock on their front door about ten minutes later.

They were soon swimming in a sea of faces. Aunts, uncles, cousins—Ryan had forgotten how much family he really had until he had to introduce them all to Kylee. She took it all like a champ, smiling and greeting everyone with her normal, happy demeanor. If Ryan didn't know any better he'd have assumed their story was real himself.

As he stood next to Kylee, watching her chat with one of his aunts about living in Denver, he momentarily gave himself the luxury of pretending it all was real. That Kylee really was his wife who loved him and he loved back. That the fingers interlocked with his weren't there for show, but because their owner really did love his touch. That all those bright smiles and comments about the life they were about to start with each other weren't a facade.

The vision was all too comfortable. He shook it from his mind and ignored the warning bells ringing in his head. He couldn't let his heart get involved in this.

A few of his family members already knew about their weekend marriage, but most were surprised to find Ryan had tied the knot.

"I never would have believed it if I hadn't seen it with my own two eyes!"

His Aunt Lucy was at least the third person to say this tonight. Ryan was starting to get a complex.

"Well, I don't know about—"

"I mean, Ryan's a great catch; there's no doubting that." She was now addressing Kylee, completely ignoring Ryan's answer. "No one could understand why a guy as wonderful as him was still single. We'd all just assumed he was the type who'd never get married." She shrugged and took a bite of the brownie on her plate.

"All I can say is I'm glad no one else snatched him up before I came along." Kylee leaned into his arm as she said this, and he instinctively pulled her closer.

The thought that he was glad no one had snatched *her* up ran through his mind.

"Aw, you two do make a cute couple," Aunt Lucy said, swallowing her last bite of brownie. "Well, excuse me, I have to go try and convince Aunt Carol to give me her brownie recipe for the hundredth time. She's been hoarding it for years, but one of these days I'm going to sneak it out of her." With that, she bustled away, her peppy aura following her like a cloud.

"Well, she's an entertaining one," Kylee said quietly when they were alone again.

Ryan smiled down at her. "Yes, as you can tell, we're a family of lively talkers." He hoped Kylee wasn't getting too overwhelmed. "Are you doing okay? I know this is a lot for the first night."

The corner of Kylee's mouth lifted, but he was pretty sure he saw some tiredness in her eyes. "Of course, I'm doing fine. Your family has all been so nice."

Her comment shouldn't have made him feel as good as it did. It wasn't like she needed to like his family or anything. But somehow, the knowledge lightened his mood.

"Ryan!"

He knew the voice before he even turned around. "Uncle Mike, how's it going?" He gave his uncle a big hug. He didn't necessarily have favorites among his aunts and uncles, but Mike was definitely one of his uncles he felt closest with. "Let me introduce you to my wife, Kylee. Kylee, this is my Uncle Mike."

"What he's trying to say is his *favorite* Uncle Mike," the large man said as he winked at Kylee.

She reached forward and shook his hand, smiling in her charming way. "Well, it's definitely a pleasure to meet the favorite uncle."

They all laughed.

"So, how have things been going?" Ryan learned it was best to initiate the discussion. It was less likely that the conversation would turn into an interrogation of him and Kylee that way.

"Eh, just the usual. Work, sports, the occasional hunt, checking off everything on Margaret's to-do list." He said this last part with another one of his trademark winks.

Margaret was Mike's wife and, subsequently, Ryan's aunt. She was a nice lady but did have the tendency to rule her house like a tight ship.

"Oh yeah?" he asked. "What'd she have you doing today?"

Uncle Mike got a sly look in his eyes. "Well, don't tell anyone, but I was supposed to stop by the house to pick up the cookies she'd left on the counter on my way here. Margaret was at a book club before this." His voice dropped low and conspiratorial. "Anyway, I forgot until I was almost here, so I just stopped by the grocery store and grabbed a pack of cookies from the bakery." His eyes glanced around. "I don't think she's noticed yet."

Ryan snorted loudly, and he could hear Kylee snickering next to him.

"I have to run to the restroom real quick," she said as their laughter died down, "but don't worry, Uncle Mike, your secret's safe with me." She gave Ryan one last smile before turning.

It wasn't until Uncle Mike cleared his throat that Ryan realized his eyes had been glued to Kylee as she walked away.

"You know," Uncle Mike said, a knowing look in his eyes, "we've always said it would take a special girl to settle you down. You've always been a bit of the ambitious type. Not the type to stop and smell the roses, if you know what I mean."

"I'm not sure whether to be offended or flattered."

"You can take it however you want. But I can tell this Kylee has caught your heart." Uncle Mike lifted his eyebrows. "I don't think your eyes have stopped following her all night long."

Ryan flushed slightly at his uncle's claim, but on the inside, his mind was racing. Had Kylee caught his heart? There was no way...right?

"Uh, yeah," Ryan coughed, trying to clear out the knot that was forming in his throat. "Well, like you said, she is a special girl."

Uncle Mike clamped him on the shoulder. "I'm just glad you weren't dumb enough to let that one get away! Now your brother, on the other hand, he could use a bit of help I think."

Ryan was only half listening to the rest of his uncle's comments. What *was* going on with him? Why were his emotions so bizarre? He'd known Kylee for how many years now, and he'd never felt any serious attraction or draw to her other than friendship. Now, as his uncle had embarrassingly pointed out, he couldn't seem to take his eyes off of her. Luckily, it would help support their story, but what was going to happen when this was all over?

Kylee found him a few minutes later and stuck to his side the rest of the night. Despite his inner turmoil, he didn't mind the company one bit.

When his extended family finally did leave, and they said their goodnights to his parents and siblings, he wordlessly reached for her hand. Without hesitation, she reached forward and allowed him to wordlessly lead her to their bedroom.

As he closed the door behind them, he leaned against it with a sigh. "Wow. Sorry about that. I didn't realize we'd be facing a firing squad so soon during this visit."

Kylee gave him a small smile. "You mean, all your family?"

He nodded. "Yeah. I knew we'd spend time with my parents and siblings tonight, but I thought we'd have another day before the extended family came to visit." He ran a hand through his hair. He hoped she realized how much he appreciated her tonight. "But you were great, seriously. Even I believed some of your answers about how amazing you thought I was." He gave her a wink, but he was being honest. He secretly wondered if any of the stuff she'd said had been true or just a part of her act.

Kylee laughed at his compliments. "What can I say, that fourth grade drama class really paid off." She yawned and stretched, and Ryan took the hint.

"You want to use the bathroom first?" He grabbed a few pillows off the bed. They had agreed that he would sleep on the floor, and she'd stay in the bed. Kylee had been reluctant to the idea, but there was really nowhere else for him to stay without alerting his family.

"Um, sure. Yeah, let me just grab some stuff." Kylee seemed a little uncertain, and Ryan didn't blame her. This had to be a little uncomfortable sharing a room with him.

He tried to give her some privacy by turning to make his makeshift bed in the far corner of the room. By the time he was satisfied with his creation, she was back, wearing a soft-looking pair of pink pajamas.

"Your turn!" she said a little too brightly, and Ryan wished there was some way he could have given her her own room for the weekend. Knowing there was no chance of that, he nodded and grabbed his own toothbrush. "Don't wait up for me," he said with a grin.

"You have a nightly facial routine or something?" she asked with raised eyebrows.

"Cleanse, exfoliate, tone, moisturize…" Ryan counted off the imaginary steps on his fingers as he turned to walk out the door.

He felt a pillow hit his back, followed by a loud, "You're ridiculous."

Ryan was glad he'd been able to lighten her mood. Hopefully, he'd taken her mind off her worries.

Now, he just wished he could do the same thing for his heart.

# Chapter 8

"Hey...Hey! Kylee…"

Kylee could hear the voice from far away but couldn't get her mind to focus. At least, not until something reached out and shook her like an earthquake.

"Wha—okay, I'm awake. What?" she exclaimed, trying to sit up and orient herself. She was surrounded by fluffy white blankets and a sea of green walls. It was only then that she remembered where she was.

She was in the green room, sleeping—or at least she had been sleeping—less than five feet from her husband. Well, her fake husband.

Ryan stood in front of her, already dressed in jeans and a sweatshirt.

"What time is it?" she mumbled as she rubbed her eyes.

"Sorry," he said in a low voice. "I know you're not a morning person. It's about six-fifteen."

"Why in heaven's name would anyone get up this early?" she grumbled as she turned to flop back on her pillow. It was true that mornings weren't her favorite, but it also hadn't helped that last night she discovered Ryan snored. The gravelly growl had kept her up for at least an hour before she finally was able to zone it out.

"Wait. Before you go back to sleep, I woke you to tell you I'm leaving."

Kylee shot straight up. "You're leaving me?"

"Not *leaving you* leaving you," he replied, laughter hinting in his voice. "I made a vow, till death do us part..."

The immediate tension his words had created dissolved into embarrassment. Why had she reacted like that? "Or at least until a trust fund payment does," she muttered, trying to cover up her inner thoughts.

He was full-on smiling now. "I'm going out to look for deer with my dad this morning. Sorry, I don't want to leave you, but this is our tradition whenever I come home."

"Look for deer?" she asked, a little confused.

"Yeah. We go drive out along some trails and scout out potential hunting spots for next season." He shrugged sheepishly. "It's kind of our thing."

Kylee nodded, clearly having never heard of such a thing. She wasn't known for her outdoorsiness, though. "Okay. What should I do?"

Ryan shrugged. "You can sleep as long as you want. Not much is happening."

She yawned. "Hmm. All right. I might go back to sleep then."

He leaned forward and kissed the top of her head, an intimate gesture that brought her fully awake.

Did Ryan just kiss her? Well, at least the top of her head? She was a little drowsy, so maybe she'd imagined it.

"Get some rest. I'll see you when I get back," he said, making no explanation for his gesture. One that he had no obligation to make since there was no one around to see.

While her mind continued whirling, Ryan walked out the door.

She lay back down, trying to forget the kiss. Really, it was barely a peck. It was a totally normal gesture for any married couple.

However, there was nothing normal about their marriage.

Kylee tried to rest for a little bit, but she never got back into a deep sleep. She spent too much time analyzing things between her and Ryan. How much of it was real, and how much of it was made-up drama in her head. After a half an hour of flopping back and forth, she finally got up.

The good thing about Ryan being gone was she could change in peace. Last night, she'd brought her PJs with her into the bathroom, hoping no one from his family would be walking by at that moment to question what she was doing.

She peeled off the warm flannel material and replaced it with jeans and a long-sleeved shirt. She kept her socks on, though. Mornings were chilly in Colorado, even in the spring. Then, she wandered slowly down the hall and into the family room and kitchen area.

Despite what Ryan had said, his mom was already awake and working in the kitchen. Kylee wandered over, figuring she could be of some help.

Becky looked up at her when she walked in. "Good morning, Kylee! How'd you sleep?"

"Oh, good. The bed is very comfortable." She shrugged. "I'm still getting used to Ryan's snoring, though." She figured this little bit of info would be great evidence as to the normalcy of their marriage.

His mom laughed as she pulled a few large bowls out of a cabinet. "He gets it from his father. They both make the same purring noise when they sleep. You'll get used to it eventually. I'm at the point where I have a hard time sleeping without it now."

Kylee laughed along with her, but inside, she couldn't help feeling like a complete imposter. What was she doing tricking all of Ryan's family? Did they really think she was the one they'd been waiting for? How would they all react when she and Ryan annulled their marriage in a month?

She pushed the thoughts aside for now. "So, what are you doing? Can I help in any way?"

Ryan's mom glanced over at her. "Sure. I'm just prepping stuff for the barbecue tonight. We have plenty of time, obviously. I just like to get things done so we can relax the rest of the day." She opened the fridge and brought out an armload of produce. "We're doing hamburgers. How are you at chopping veggies?"

"Well, I've never been professionally trained, but I think I'm decent enough," Kylee said, rolling up her sleeves.

"Perfect." Becky slid the cutting board over to Kylee's side of the counter with a knife on top of it. "Why don't you start slicing tomatoes? We just need quarter-inch slices to go on top of the burgers."

As Kylee began slicing, Ryan's mom got out ground beef and began shaping patties.

"So, tell me more about you and Ryan. I can't help wondering. You know he's never told us any details other than what he said last night. We had no idea." She didn't say this accusingly, more just pointing out the facts.

Still, Kylee steeled herself for another conversation of lies. "He's a funny one, isn't he? Let's see..." She racked her brain, trying to remember the fake dates they'd made up in the car. "Our first date was to a farmer's market just around the corner from me..." She spent the next ten minutes mixing fact with fiction as she told their history.

Ryan's mom was all smiles while she was talking. It was clear she was pleased to see her son so happy.

Midway through Kylee's storytelling, Ryan's grandma walked in. She didn't say anything, just sat on the stool next to Kylee and began tearing apart heads of lettuce as she listened.

Their little trio felt so natural as they worked.

As Kylee finished telling their engagement story, she asked, "So, tell me about Ryan when he was little. Was he the same as he is now?" She placed the sliced tomatoes on the large platter in front of her.

Becky gave a little laugh as her gaze met his grandma's. "I guess you could say so. Ryan was probably the most stubborn and determined little boy who ever lived."

"When he was four years old, he came knocking on my door, asking if I had a bike he could borrow," his grandma broke in. "I did, but it was an old rusty one that was about two sizes too big for him."

"Why did he need the bike?" Kylee asked.

"Because I told him he was too little to ride a bike without training wheels, and I wouldn't remove them from his bike," his mom continued. "I should've known better. Ryan insisted he could and decided to take matters into his own hands. He taught himself to ride on that rusty old thing and was proud as a peacock as he rode it in front of me two days later."

"Albeit with a body full of scratches and bruises from all the times he'd fallen," his grandma added dryly.

Kylee laughed. "That does sound like Ryan."

They spent the next twenty minutes retelling old family stories that kept Kylee laughing nonstop.

Just as they were finishing, Madison walked into the kitchen, still in her PJs. "What'd I miss?" she asked sleepily.

"Not much," her mom answered, "just filling Kylee in on some stories about your brother."

When Madison noticed Kylee, she straightened a little. "I see. I guess you probably would need a little help learning about your husband," she said pointedly, emphasizing the last words. "Seeing as you've known each other for such a short time."

Madison's mom looked at her with confused eyes before Madison swiftly changed the subject.

"What time is everyone coming over today? I was planning on meeting one of my old girlfriends for lunch today."

"I think we're planning to eat at five," Becky said. "I'm sure everyone will show up around four. That should give you plenty of time to see her."

Madison nodded and went over to the walk-in pantry.

"Why don't you grab the cereal out for everyone?" Ryan's mom called over her shoulder. She turned and faced Kylee. "I hope you don't mind. We're just having cereal for breakfast."

Kylee just waved her off. "Cereal's fine. I eat it every day."

"So Kylee, what do you do for work?" Ryan's grandma asked, her penetrating look now focused on Kylee.

"Well, the bulk of my time is spent doing freelance designing. It was what I was doing for Ryan when we first met." Kylee took one of the additional bowls Madison had pulled out as she talked. "I also work at the library a couple days a week, too, just for a little steady income."

"That's a smart approach," his grandma said matter-of-factly. "Do you think you'll continue working after you and Ryan have children?"

"I, uh...haven't really thought about it...yet." Kylee knew she was stuttering but couldn't help it. How should she have answered that? She and Ryan hadn't gone over answers for questions about their future. They'd been solely concerned about covering their fake history.

His grandma's eyes narrowed, and Kylee focused on the cereal she was pouring. It wasn't until her bowl was full that she realized she'd been holding a box of Raisin Bran. Definitely not her first pick, but it was too late now.

"I used to work as a dental assistant myself before we had children. I miss it sometimes," Becky said, filling the silence.

"You know you could've gone back, Mom," Madison said as she sat down with her bowl. "We would've been fine with a babysitter occasionally."

"I know, but I don't regret my decision. I loved those years, staying home with you all."

Kylee thought about what her future would have been if she and Ryan were married for real. Would she have quit working when they had kids? Would they have even had kids? What would it have been like to sit with Ryan and discuss these real-life questions instead of just fake, hypothetical ones?

"So, how long does looking for deer take?" Kylee asked, hoping she was using the term correctly.

Becky laughed, a soft, musical noise compared to the hearty laugh Ryan and his father shared. "That is always a good question. Depending on if they actually find something, it could take them all morning." She gave Kylee a wink. "But since Ryan knows you're back here waiting for him, I'm sure they'll be home in an hour or two."

"I don't know how they last that long," Madison responded, rolling her eyes. "After ten minutes, I am bored out of my mind."

"Which is why they no longer invite you to ride along," her mom said as she began wiping the counter down.

Kylee finished her bowl of cereal, choking down the raisins as quickly as she could. "I might go explore a little bit, unless you need more help?" she asked.

Becky shook her head. "No, go ahead. But bring a jacket. It's cold out there."

Kylee smiled at the motherly suggestion.

"There's a nice trail right off the backyard," Becky continued. "It goes on for miles, but if you follow it about half a mile up, there's a pretty viewpoint of the valley."

Kylee nodded her thanks. "Okay. I'll head that way, then."

She grabbed her jacket from the room since moms always knew best. Then, she was off to enjoy some much-needed alone time.

*****

By the time Ryan, his dad, and his brother got back, it was late morning. He walked in the door, for some reason expecting Kylee to be there waiting for him with open arms.

Instead, all he got was his mom reading in the corner and his grandma crocheting in the family room.

"Where's Kylee?" he asked, searching the room.

"I knew it. She took the first opportunity to run," Mason said behind him, rubbing his hands together to warm up.

Ryan scoffed. "You're probably right, but it's because she found out she was stuck with you for a brother-in-law for the rest of her life."

"You two," Ryan's mom said. "She went for a walk on the back trail about thirty minutes ago. She should be home soon. You might be able to catch her if you head out that way."

Ryan nodded and went straight out the back door. He was surprised at the disappointment he'd felt at not seeing her. Waking up that morning had been different, and not just because he'd been sleeping on the floor. Seeing Kylee snuggled warmly in the bed had given him strange feelings. Feelings of contentment and almost longing. He'd wondered what it would have been like to wake up every morning seeing her. More specifically, what it would have been like waking up actually next to her, instead of on the floor.

He thought about this as he made his way out to the trail, dead pine needles crunching under his shoes. The weather wasn't freezing, but it was at least in the mid-50s. He shoved his hands into his pockets to keep them warm.

Ryan had walked this trail many times over the last few years. It was one of his mom's favorite haunts, and he often joined her in the early mornings whenever he'd visit. He wondered how Kylee liked it.

After ten minutes, he finally rounded the bend right before the lookout point. Kylee came into view, squatting low on the ground with her phone in front of her, taking pictures. He watched her for a few minutes in silence.

Every couple of seconds, she changed her position and moved her camera to a different angle. She wasn't taking typical scenic shots. She was getting pictures from all different points—down low behind a rock, up high next to the tree branches. He wondered what the purpose of these were.

Not wanting to startle her, he called out from ten feet away. "Hey, pretty lady. What are you doing out here?"

She spun around, her eyes wide. "Ryan! How did you find me?"

He tried not to laugh. "Well, you are standing on the main trail that goes past my parents' backyard. And my mom told me where you'd gone. It wasn't too hard."

Her worry lines slowly eased, and she smiled. "Of course."

He approached until they were shoulder to shoulder, staring out over the valley. "So, what are you taking pictures of?"

She blushed a little. “Nothing specific. It’s just such a beautiful scene. I wanted to capture it.”

“Did you bring any of your camera equipment?” he asked.

“No, I didn’t think I needed it. But I’m regretting it now.” She held her phone up. “Luckily, this thing actually has a decent lens, so I got a few fun shots.”

He took her phone and swiped through some of the photos she’d taken. They were beautiful. She’d managed to set the scene in so many different perspectives.

Once he’d seen them all, he handed the phone back to her. “You are so talented—seriously. There’s much more to you than you let most people see.” In his heart, he knew he was talking about more than just her photography skills, but he tried to keep his tone light.

She lifted her face to the sun with a smile. “Thanks. That means a lot coming from you.”

“Coming from me?” He tilted his head to the side.

“Yeah, you’re not someone who gives out compliments lightly. I know you mean what you say. So, thank you.”

He put his arm around her companionably, a gesture he wouldn’t have done even three days ago. Somehow, the last twenty-four hours had brought them closer, though.

They stood there, enjoying the view and the company.

Eventually, Ryan’s stomach let out a loud growl and interrupted the moment. “Well, if you haven’t guessed, I’m actually pretty hungry. You ready to head back?”

"Sure," she laughed. "I'd hate to starve you out here." She turned and started walking back down the trail, the warmth cuddled under his arm gone.

As she headed away from him, a pang hit his heart. Despite his hunger, he wished he would have starved a little longer so he could have spent a little more time alone with her. Some more time just being together.

The question was, what did that even mean?

# Chapter 9

As Becky said, everyone showed up to the house around four. Kylee was sure the crowd had multiplied from yesterday. There were definitely more kids running around, at least.

No one else seemed ruffled by the horde of people, though. However, no one else was getting interrogated quite like she and Ryan were, either.

"You got married last week?"

"You didn't even tell your parents?"

"How long had you two been dating?"

"When are you going to start having kids?"

The barrage of questions was never-ending. Kylee tried to stay close to Ryan the whole time. That way, she could deflect most of the inquiries to him. But eventually, he got roped into helping grill the burgers, so she was left to fend for herself.

Somehow, she got stuck in a conversation with some of his aunts about pregnancy horrors. After hearing her fourth story about epidural failures, she excused herself to go to the bathroom.

Kylee slowly washed her hands and then splashed water on her face, wishing she could have fast-forwarded through this night. Actually, this whole week.

It wasn't that she didn't like Ryan's family. It was quite the opposite. They were a fun group of people who had welcomed her with arms wide open. It was the knowledge that she was lying to them all that did it.

She hated smiling and telling them to their faces that, yes, she was deeply in love with Ryan. Yes, their marriage had been a dream so far. No, they hadn't talked about kids, but she was sure they'd have them soon. Lies. Lies. Lies.

Well, all but one.

This wasn't who she was. Not that she was perfect, but she liked to think she was generally an honest person. And all this acting just felt wrong.

Straightening her shoulders, she re-hung the hand towel. She had chosen this. She'd known what she was getting herself into, and now, she needed to see it through to the end. Ryan was counting on her, and as an added bonus, her future debt-free self would be thankful as well.

Kylee left the bathroom, determined to put on a good act. As she glanced out the family room window, she saw a flurry of motion. Out in the yard, Ryan was jumping around, chasing a few little boys who couldn't have been older than five or six. She watched them for a few minutes, concluding that they were playing some sort of game of tag. When he finally let one of the boys catch him, it hit her that this could be her future. That could be her husband outside, playing with her children.

Ryan would make a great dad. Sure, he wasn't perfect, but she'd always known he had a good heart. That was why she'd fallen for him in the first place.

She sucked in a deep breath, willing the determination she'd felt moments ago to return. Ryan was only her husband for a month. This wasn't a long-term thing. This wasn't even a real thing. She was being paid to do a job.

With her shoulders squared, she stepped away from the window and turned back toward the crowd.

*****

Ryan came back inside the house, looking for his wife—he made a quick course correction—looking for Kylee. He'd lost her in the crowd. When he finally found her, she was chatting with a group of his older cousins, surprisingly looking like she was enjoying herself.

Everything about Kylee was so bright and fresh. She was constantly interested in everybody and everything. He studied her features, admiring her high cheekbones and the slight flush to her face. Her green eyes were always captivating, but never more so than when she was excited about something.

He realized how beautiful she was in an unsuspecting way. She wasn't the type of girl to stop a party when she entered, but when you gave her a second glance, you couldn't look away.

But now wasn't the time for that. Just a few more days, then they'd go back home, wait out the rest of the month, and get their annulment. Staying married to him for real had never been part of the deal.

The thought made him swallow hard to relieve the pit in his stomach. He had to keep his eye on the prize: making sure his family believed in their marriage. He grinned a little to himself. There was nothing wrong with making sure he put on a good show for them, though, right?

Sneaking behind Kylee, he slowly wrapped his arms around her waist, leaning to talk directly into her ear. She jumped a little at the sound of his voice.

"How are you doing?" His low voice vibrated against the side of her face. He couldn't help being pleased at the goosebumps that rippled across her skin.

"Good," she said quietly.

Ryan flicked his gaze over her shoulder and noticed the others in the circle glancing at them. Kylee must have, too, because she turned to face him and wrapped her arms loosely around his waist.

At that, the resolve he'd made to himself moments ago flew from his mind. Ryan wanted nothing more than to be alone with Kylee, snuggled on the couch, not worrying about what all of his family was thinking about them and their hoax of a marriage. He tightened his grip on her, bringing her body even closer.

*Clap! Clap! Clap!*

The moment was interrupted by his mother clapping to get everyone's attention. When only half the room turned around, his dad took matters into his own hands.

"Hey, everyone," he said in a voice that didn't need the help of a microphone.

The chatter in the room immediately stopped, and all eyes turned toward the front.

"Thank you," Ryan's mom said, trying to bite back a smile. "I'm so grateful you all came to join us this night. It's so good to be together with family."

She paused for a moment and found Ryan in the crowd. "I'd also like to formally welcome the newest member of our family, Kylee!"

Every eye in the room shifted to Kylee. She stiffened under his arm, probably from the sudden onslaught of unwanted attention. He gave her a squeeze of support, and his thumb stroked a rhythmic pattern on her shoulder, trying to relax her.

"You are the perfect surprise this week, and I couldn't be happier to call you my daughter-in-law," his mom continued. "There came a point where I began to give up hope of Ryan marrying, but I can see now he was just waiting for the perfect girl."

There was a chorus of "Hear, hear!" and clapping at the end of her little speech.

Kylee's face had drained of color, but she had a determined smile fixed on her face. Ryan kept his arm wrapped around her, both as a demonstration of affection and as a way to keep her standing.

"Thank you, everyone," he said, waving as he spoke. "We're happy to be here, too."

There were more cheers until the focus slowly started to fade away from the newly married couple, and everyone went back to their conversations.

Ryan still had his death grip on Kylee since she felt like she was about to slump over at any second. He looked down at her. "Are you okay?" he asked softly.

She turned her robotic smile onto him. "Yes, just feeling a little guilty about all this."

He nodded. "I'm sorry, I didn't know my mom was going to do that."

"It's fine. Really, it is." She took a deep breath. "Want to go grab a cookie?" She indicated toward the large platter of desserts on the kitchen counter.

"Of course. Sugar makes everything better," Ryan replied with a smile.

As he turned to walk over to the kitchen, he almost stumbled over Madison standing right behind them. She gave them both a narrow-eyed look before rushing past.

Ryan wasn't sure what that was about but shrugged it off. He was ready for this night to be over.

*****

Most of the partygoers finally left around nine. Kylee had mentally tapped out after Becky's little toast. She still smiled and joined in the group conversations, but she no longer took an active role in meeting and speaking with everyone.

Due to her mental exhaustion, she had no problem zoning out Ryan's snores that night. And the next morning, since Ryan didn't wake her, she didn't come out of her coma-like state until almost eight thirty.

When the sunlight filtering through the half-closed blinds did finally rouse her, she rolled over in a slow stretch. Peeking at the floor, she noted the empty pile of blankets. How long had Ryan been up?

After grabbing her phone, she turned on the selfie camera to inspect what she had to work with. She'd forgotten to take her makeup off the night before, so she had smudged black circles under her eyes. A haphazard crisscross of pillow lines covered her left cheek as well. Mostly, though, she just looked tired. Not in a lack-of-sleep way; more in a stressed-out-over-life way.

Sighing, she stripped out of her pajamas and put on jeans and a cozy sweater. After that, she went to the bathroom to wash her face and brush her teeth. Feeling a little more like a human being, she walked down the hall to see where the rest of the family was. A savory smell wafted toward her, and when she reached the family room, she saw the spread of breakfast food out on the counter.

"Hey...babe," Ryan called from the couch. His comment was slightly stilted, but she doubted anyone else noticed.

She smiled, mentally pretending they were back at his condo and there was no one else around. "Hey. Thanks for letting me sleep in. What smells so good?"

He grabbed her hand, pulling her down next to him on the couch."My mom made her famous French toast with eggs, and sausage, and who knows what else. I think she forgot that the extended family left and there's only us this morning." He spoke loud enough so his mom could hear from the kitchen, but his focus seemed to still be on her, as if he were trying to reassure her that it was just them and they could relax for a little while. "She made enough food for an army."

"With the way you and your brother eat, you might as well be an army," his mom retorted without missing a beat.

Kylee snickered and relaxed against Ryan, tucking her feet up under her. "It smells delicious. I'll have to go get some in a minute." She didn't want to get up just yet. She loved being nestled into the crook of Ryan's arm. He was warm and smelled like soap and aftershave. She had to hold herself back from digging her face into his chest and inhaling deeply.

"So," Ryan continued, absently beginning to play with her hair, "what do you want to do today? I was thinking something outdoorsy would be in order."

Kylee nodded into his side. "Sounds good. Whatever you'd normally be doing works for me."

"First, I have to help my dad load some wood in the truck."

"Wood for what?"

"For a job site he's working on."

She poked her head up for a second. "A job site?"

Ryan smiled down at her. "Yeah, didn't I mention he's a general contractor?"

Kylee shook her head, his shoulder limiting her movement.

"My dad has been a contractor his whole life—mostly home projects like custom designs, kitchen remodels, etc." He laughed, the sound vibrating through his chest to her head. "I was more often than not on his grunt crew. My jobs generally included things like loading the dumpster, moving supplies...really important things."

"Clearly, your dad didn't show his sons any favoritism."

"Nope. If anything, he took the opposite approach. He thought giving us the hard jobs would build character."

"Well, isn't that how you got that six-pack you were bragging to Mason about?" She poked him playfully in the stomach, not at all surprised when her finger hit a solid wall of muscle.

"Well, if you think my six-pack is impressive, you should see my biceps." He lifted his free arm and began flexing in an exaggerated way, bringing Kylee into a fit of giggles.

"You're ridiculous," she cried. She loved the easy way he took her teasing.

He grinned down at her, and she swore there was an instant where his eyes landed on her lips and froze.

"So, um, how long will this load take?" she asked, sitting up. She gained a sudden awareness for how close they were sitting.

"Forty-five minutes at most. It would have been faster if Mason was here to help." Ryan let out a yawn. "But he had to go into Denver for a couple days for work. He should be back on Sunday.  You can use the time to eat and put on your hiking boots. We'll head out when I get back."

"That works. Although, my running shoes will have to do, because I don't have any hiking boots."

"What?" he responded as they stood up together. "My wife has to own a pair of hiking boots. We'll have to remedy that soon."

Kylee smiled at him but, inside, was processing his comment. Was he saying that just because his family was around? Trying to play up their marriage act? Or was there an underlying intent to it? Meanwhile, Ryan was heading for his shoes near the back door.

"Hey, Mom, I'm going out to help Dad. Anything you need me to tell him?" Ryan asked as he tied his laces.

"No, just make sure he's careful with his back. He threw it out about two weeks ago but is too stubborn to lay off it," his mom answered with a sigh.

"I can't make any promises, but I'll tell him," Ryan said with a shrug. He headed for the door then turned and backtracked to Kylee.

She stood, holding her empty plate, watching his approach curiously.

"Can't leave without a goodbye kiss from my wife," he said. He leaned forward, turning at the last second so his kiss landed on her cheek instead of her mouth. With a slightly flushed face, he headed out the door.

Kylee tried to gather her wits and act like the kiss was normal. If you could have even called it a kiss, really. He could've given the same gesture to his grandma.

She absentmindedly began filling a plate with food. When she finally looked down at it, she realized she had taken enough for at least two people. It did all look really good, though. "I'm going to leave here ten pounds heavier," she said to Becky, who was leaning on the counter, reading the newspaper ads.

"With a body like yours, you could add ten pounds and no one would notice," she said over the edge of the paper.

Kylee smiled before she took a seat at the table. She dug into her breakfast, the food tasting as good as it smelled.

Just as she was scooping up the last of the eggs, her phone started vibrating in her pocket. When she pulled it out, the screen flashed with *Elena*. She silenced the call and then hopped out of her chair. While rinsing her plate off, she said, "I think I'm going to take a walk outside for a few minutes. I'll be back in a bit."

Becky, absorbed in her newspaper, just nodded.

Kylee grabbed a jacket from her room and went out the back door, already dialing Elena's number as she walked.

"*Hermana*! Are you alive?" Elena's voice was such a welcome sound. It felt like it had been weeks since she'd talked to her roommate, instead of days.

"Barely. I feel like, any second, someone's going to jump out and call me out as the fraud I am." Kylee circled the house as she talked, not even noticing where she was going.

"Are they treating you bad? Say the word, girl, and you know I'm there."

Elena's feistiness always made Kylee laugh.

"No, no, I'm fine," she assured her friend. "I really am. Ryan's family is actually super nice. I can't complain about them at all. It's just the whole lying aspect I can't deal with. It almost makes it worse that everyone is so nice. I feel like such a bad person." She peered around to make sure no one was listening.

"How is Ryan handling it?"

"He seems fine—better than me. I honestly believe him most of the time and forget I'm not really his wife. He's so good at playing at it." She had made her way around to the front of the house and decided to lounge in one of the oversized rockers on the porch.

"Maybe he's not playing at it," was Elena's blunt reply.

Kylee rolled her eyes. "Elena, we've been over this. Ryan has no feelings for me. He never has and never will. All his hand-holding and sweet-talking to me is just an act."

"So he's holding your hand a lot?"

"Yes—no. I mean, not a lot. Just a normal amount."

"Could you define 'sweet talking' too? Like, is he calling you babe and telling you how *bonita* your eyes are—"

"We're only doing this so he can fund his business, Elena," Kylee hissed through clenched teeth. "That is it."

"I feel like you're being defensive. Are you sure there's not more to this than you're telling me? Are you developing stronger feelings for him?"

"No, of course not!" Kylee's reply sounded forced even to her own ears. "Look, I respect Ryan. He's a great guy and has many admirable qualities—"

"Including a fantastic bod, great eyes—"

"Including a kind and courteous heart that would never let him play with a girl's emotions. Which is why I guarantee he feels nothing for me but friendship. And I'm going to leave it at that."

"Has he kissed you again?"

Even in the spring chill, Kylee's skin flared with warmth. "That's it. I'm hanging up."

Elena's laughter forced Kylee to purse her lips to stop from smiling herself. She could have never truly been mad at her best friend.

"Fine, fine. I'll let it be. So his family is super nice, Ryan is super amazing, and everything is wonderful except for the guilt you feel about this little charade."

"Basically," Kylee said with a deep sigh. "I guess I can't complain. It could be a lot worse."

"Yes, but that doesn't mean this is easy. I'm sorry," Elena said. "Wish I could make things better. If it's any consolation, you're going to get your school loans paid off at the end of this."

"You're right," she agreed, rubbing her forehead with the back of her palm. "I just need to think about it from that perspective. This is a business arrangement. I just need to fulfill my end of the bargain, and everything will be good."

"And you need to make sure you don't lose your heart to Ryan in the process."

Kylee's breath locked up in her chest at that thought. She couldn't think about it, so she rushed to end the phone call. "Goodbye, Elena."

Her roommate giggled a little. "Bye, Kylee. Love ya."

"Love you, too." Kylee hung up, somehow feeling better and worse at the same time. Even across the phone, Elena could tell Kylee was falling harder for Ryan. She needed to do a better job at emotionally distancing herself from him.

Sighing, she stood and stretched. The view was gorgeous, but it was time to get back inside so she could get ready for her fake husband's return. She made her way to the front door and placed her shoes, wet from the grass, outside to dry.

As she shut the door, movement to her right caught her eye. There, sitting on the couch just underneath the front window, was Ryan's grandma, silently knitting away.

Kylee's gut clenched. Had she heard Kylee's phone call? The chair Kylee had been sitting on was a few feet away from that window on the porch. How soundproof were the windows?

The one person who needed to believe Kylee and Ryan's fake marriage was his grandma. It was her trust money that Ryan needed, after all.

Clenching her teeth, Kylee stepped quietly away from the door, hoping she hadn't blown the entire thing. She entered the room, not sure what she was going to say but needing to know the truth.

"What are you making?" she asked, sitting on the edge of the loveseat.

Ryan's grandma glanced over at her, her hands never ceasing their knitting motion. "Kylee, I didn't see you there. I'm making a blanket for one of the neighbor's daughters. She's having her first baby, and there's nothing like a knitted blanket for warmth." Her eyes went back to her needlework.

"Well, it's lovely," Kylee agreed. "I'm sure she's going to love it."

His grandma gave her a smile. "I hope so, because these hands don't knit as quickly as they used to."

Kylee just barely bit back asking if her ears heard as good as they used to as well. She fidgeted for a moment, rubbing her hands down her jeans. "Well, I better go see if Ryan's back. We're going on a little hike."

This time, his grandma's hands stopped, and she placed her work on her lap. "That's a great idea. There's nothing quite like quality time spent with the ones you love." Her eyebrows rose, almost in question.

Kylee nodded, the pit in her stomach growing heavier.

She didn't know what to think. Either Ryan's grandma really hadn't heard her conversation with Elena, or she had one of the world's best poker faces out there.

# Chapter 10

Something seemed off with Kylee when Ryan returned a few minutes later. Had it been his goodbye kiss? He'd planned to give her a full mouth kiss, then, at the last second, chickened out. Something about her recently set his nerves on fire.

He helped her get her coat on as they reached the front door, trying to determine if he should ask her about it.

Before he could say anything, though, she stepped outside, turning and cocking an eyebrow when he didn't follow. "You coming?" she asked.

"Yeah," he said, spurring into motion. When she headed toward his car, he grabbed her elbow. "We'll actually be borrowing my dad's truck this morning. The trail we're going to is a little off the beaten path."

Kylee just shrugged and headed toward the truck. The truck was old, made sometime in the 1970s, but it had character—like a squeaky passenger door that made its presence known as Kylee got in.

Ryan jumped into the driver's seat. "Now, the key to getting this thing started is you have to pump the gas pedal three times before you try the ignition." He grinned at Kylee as he inserted the keys into the ignition. "Don't ask me why. I just know it won't work otherwise."

She laughed. "And do I have to click my heels three times to get the heater working?"

He put the car in reverse and began backing up. "Yep. Then you have to say the magic words." After he pulled out of the driveway, he turned the heat on high, purposely aiming the center vents at her. "Just kidding. The heat is the one thing in this truck that actually works pretty well."

As his hands were kept occupied, shifting the car into the different gears, his mind was free to notice the air of tension around her again. "So, how are you really doing? This is the first time we've been able to chat without someone eavesdropping." The car protested as he put it into fourth gear, but eventually it cooperated.

Kylee seemed to flinch at the word *eavesdropping*. She cleared her throat. "I'm okay. All this lying is kind of getting to me. I'm usually a pretty straightforward kind of girl."

Ryan felt his shoulders droop a little. This was the last thing he wanted Kylee to be feeling. "I know, and I really love that about you. I'm sorry I'm making you go against your morals." Hold up. Did he just say love? Out loud?

He cleared his throat and went on to cover his gaffe. "If it makes you feel better, I don't like it any more myself.

Every time my grandma asks me a question, I feel her eyes boring into me. I'm always on the verge of blurting out the truth." He gave her a sheepish look. "When I was a kid, I was convinced she had an internal lie detector. She always seemed to know when I was in trouble." He tried to relax his hands on the steering wheel, his fingers just slightly uncurling themselves.

Kylee tucked a stray hair behind her ear.

"You know you don't have to do this, Kylee. We can go home right now if you want. You know I'd never hold it against you." He glanced at her. "I can always make up some sort of excuse. You caught the chicken pox or something."

She laughed and looked over at him with raised eyebrows. "I'm not sure if you're aware, but no one gets the chicken pox anymore." She turned and looked out the passenger window, almost like she was trying to avoid his eyes. "Don't worry about me. I'm a big girl and can take care of myself," she finally said.

There was a lull in their conversation after that. There was obviously something on her mind, but Ryan didn't want to keep bugging her about it.

"So, where are you taking me?"

Her questions pulled him out of his thoughts. He let out a slow breath, both happy for a new subject but a little sad that they didn't seem to resolve anything. "It's a trail I used to hike a bunch as a kid. It's not too far, maybe three miles round-trip, but it leads to an amazing waterfall."

"Really?" Kylee asked. "What's the name of it? Is it well-known?"

Ryan let out a hearty laugh, knowing Kylee was in for a surprise. "There's a reason we're driving this truck. It's not one of the more well-traveled paths."

"I'm not going to fall off a cliff or get eaten by a bear or anything, am I?"

Ryan reached across the cab and took her hand in his, linking their fingers. "Don't worry, wife. I'll take care of you." He had meant to say this as a joke, but the humor was lost the instant their fingers connected. All he could think about was how good her hand felt in his, and how wrong that feeling should have been.

*****

As Ryan had said, the trail was quite a ways off the main road. After driving down a dirt path for at least a mile, he parked the truck. Kylee got out and glanced around them, trying for the life of her to find the trailhead.

"Um, so, where are we going?" she asked, peering around.

Ryan just smiled and pointed to her left. "See that big tree? Right behind it, the trail starts."

She waved a hand. "I'll let you lead the way."

They started walking in a line, the trail only wide enough to allow one person at a time. Ryan went first, as

Kylee had suggested, being sure to point out any rocks or tree stumps she should avoid.

About a quarter-mile into the hike, the trail started ascending. And it stayed that way the rest of their hike.

"You didn't mention…we would be walking up...a mountain," Kylee huffed when they stopped for a break. She wasn't a professional athlete, by any means, but she was in decent enough shape. She ran at least twice a week and occasionally did a yoga video if she was really motivated. But there was something about mountain elevation and dirt trails that took the wind out of her. She unzipped her jacket and tied it around her waist.

She noticed Ryan's cheeks were a little flushed too, but his breathing was still normal. "Well, if you want to see a waterfall, that means you have to go up."

She straightened. "All right, wise guy." She took a swig of the water he'd offered and handed it back. "I'm good now."

"Don't worry. We probably only have about ten more minutes until we're there." He started walking again, slowing his pace slightly, which she appreciated.

"So, you like to do this kind of thing with a pack on your back? And for several days in a row?" she asked the back of his head.

"You know it," he answered, true excitement in his voice. "There's nothing as fun as a good backpacking trip."

"I can think of a couple of things," she mumbled, thinking about the book she'd yet to crack open back at the house.

"What was that?" he called back.

"Nothing. So,"—she stepped over a thick root, changing the subject—"how long are your hikes, usually?"

"Some guys like to go out for nine or ten days at a time. But that's not my style. I like a good three-or-four-day trip. Just long enough to get into nature and forget about everything, but not so long that I have to carry a heavy pack."

"What do you mean?"

"Well, you have to carry all the food you plan to eat. The more days you're out there, the more food you have to carry," Ryan answered.

"Oh, that makes sense," Kylee said, feeling a little dumb. "I guess that's also why having a light backpack is so important."

He turned around and gave her a little grin. "Exactly. The dyneema composite fabric Hudson bags are supposed to be made of is extremely lightweight. Yet another reason why my backpacks are going to be so awesome—if they ever get into production."

"Have you heard anything about the trust fund yet?" She was beginning to huff again, but talking distracted her, so she tried to keep the conversation going.

"Yeah," he answered over his shoulder. "I spoke to my bank yesterday, and they said the transfer should come in before this weekend, which would be awesome, because I told my manufacturer I'd get him the funds before Monday." He lifted his hands high to show his crossed fingers. "If everything goes as planned, we should be in production by early next week."

"That's...awesome..." Kylee couldn't talk any more. Luckily for her, Ryan stopped abruptly.

"We're here." He faced her. "So, to get to the actual outlook spot, we have to walk along a ledge. It's not too narrow, maybe about a foot or so, but you have to be careful."

"A foot?" Kylee squeaked out. It wasn't that she was overly scared of heights, but a one-foot ledge on the side of a mountain certainly didn't sound appealing.

"You'll be fine—trust me. I'll be there with you the whole time. Just follow me and do what I do." His confidence only slightly reassured her.

He continued down the path, which jolted to the left. They went down a tiny slope for another ten feet. Then, the treeline opened up and, as Ryan had said, there was a one-and-a-half-foot ledge they had to walk across to get to a wide overhang. She could hear the roar of water, obviously from the waterfall she couldn't see yet.

"All right," Ryan said. "I'm going to go first. I'll be right on the other side. Once you're halfway, you'll be able to reach my hand, and I'll help you along." When she didn't say anything, he turned to peer at her. Her attempt to look composed clearly didn't work. "Kylee," he said, his voice suddenly quiet, “you don’t have to do this if you don’t want to. It’s totally your choice.”

She blinked rapidly at him. Suddenly, she was no longer thinking about crossing this ledge. Ryan had said those exact same words to her less than an hour ago about pretending to be his wife. He wasn’t going to force Kylee to do anything she didn’t want to. It was her choice. Did she want to take the risk and see what could happen? Or did she want to play it safe?

“I’m ready. Let’s do this,” was her adamant reply.

Ryan stared at her for another second before nodding. “Okay. Like I said, wait for me to cross. I’ll call you when it’s your turn.”

He squeezed her hands, and then he was off. Kylee swallowed, her hands trembling at the loss of Ryan’s.

With surprising speed, Ryan took four quick leaps and crossed the ledge. Kylee could see him on the other side, staring back at her.

The roar of the unseen waterfall emphasized the distance between them. He cupped his hands around his mouth and then called, “Your turn!”

Kylee's heart pounded in her chest, but she stepped forward. She wasn’t going to let her fears rule her life.

With her body facing the rock wall, she stepped out onto the ledge. In comparison to Ryan’s confident, large strides, hers were tiny shuffles along the ledge. But in less than a minute, she was well over halfway, and Ryan reached his hand out toward her.

"Here, I got you. You did it." His voice soothed her, and for a second, she lifted her eyes from the rock to him.

His arm was outstretched, less than a foot or two from her. She reached her hand out and felt a solid tug pulling her toward him. Next thing she knew, she was in his arms on the other side, and he was smiling down at her. The contrast of hugging the cold, stone wall compared to his warm, protective body was like night and day.

"See, that wasn't so bad," he said softly.

No. It wasn't so bad if this was the outcome. It wasn't hard to be in Ryan's arms. In fact, she could get used to this. Early morning breakfasts with him, hikes in the afternoon… Maybe even one of those multi-day hikes he'd been talking about earlier. She wouldn't have minded spending more time with him alone.

She watched as his gaze trailed her face. When his dark eyes landed on her lips, she froze. Was he going to kiss her? Like a magnet, she felt pulled toward him. There was a split second pause before they started drawing together when—

*Tap-tap-tap-tap-tap-tap!*

Kylee jumped, and it was a good thing Ryan was holding on to her or she would've come way too close to the edge.

"What the—" she exclaimed.

They both looked up into the trees where the noise was coming from. At first, neither of them could see anything, but then Ryan pointed.

"There, see him on that branch? It's a woodpecker."

Kylee put a hand over her eyes. "He scared the daylights out of me," she said, trying to bite back the disappointment of the missed kiss.

"Yeah, me too..." Ryan's comment trailed off as he gazed back at Kylee. When she caught him staring, he cleared his throat. "Well, looks like we both made it safely. Better check out that waterfall we came for."

As he said that, everything came back into focus. Kylee's ears felt like they'd unplugged, and she could hear the thundering water again.

Ryan turned, and Kylee glanced behind him before drawing in a breath of shock. It was one of the most stunning things she'd ever seen in her life. The water spewed off the edge of a fifty-foot cliff before it free-fell into a pool below. The rocks had been cut and formed by the water over the years to the point that they had smooth, glasslike edges.

"Because it's early spring, there's a ton more water from all the melting snow," Ryan explained. "If we came here at the end of summer, it wouldn't be quite so magnificent."

"I can't imagine this being anything but magnificent," Kylee replied, her mouth still hanging open.

He just smiled. "I'm glad you came all the way. It would've been a pity if you'd missed this." He reached down and grabbed her hand, cupping it in both of his.

Kylee smiled and thought about what she would've missed if she had stayed back. The view. The waterfall. This time alone with Ryan.

Similarly, she thought about what she would have missed had she not agreed to this marriage. She had learned so much about him in the last few days, more than she'd ever thought she would have. Ryan had exceeded her expectations in all areas. Seeing him with his family, the way he interacted with his mother and his sister, and even his grandma… It all gave her a glimpse of the deeper sides of him.

Even things like this moment at the waterfall, simply holding his hand and enjoying the beauty of nature, would have been missed.

"You know," Ryan said, interrupting the silence, "when I was a teenager, I used to come here all the time. This was my calming spot when I was whining about the unfairness of life."

"Unfairness of life?" Kylee asked, suppressing a smile.

"Yeah, you know. The real deep things. Like the time my mom wouldn't let me go to a party, or when Coach didn't put me in for the final play of the game." He grinned down at her. "You're the first person I've ever taken to this spot, actually."

He'd said the comment casually, but the words held a deep meaning. She was the first person he'd brought to this spot? Clearly, it was important to him, but why had he felt the need to bring her there?

She looked down and noticed their hands were still entwined in a tight grasp. Whether on purpose or absentmindedly, Ryan's thumb was slowly stroking the edge of her wrist. She glanced up at him to find his gaze steadily fixed on hers.

"Kylee, I know this whole marriage is a fake. I know you don't really have feelings for me, and we already agreed to annul it when the month is up," Ryan said, looking down to focus on the toe of his shoe as he dug it into the dirt. "I just...I keep getting these crazy—"

*Tap-tap-tap-tap-tap-tap!*

His monologue was interrupted by the woodpecker, who had apparently given up on his previous tree and was now pecking at one just above their heads. Kylee was about ready to strangle the bird.

Ryan dropped her hand at the noise and ran his fingers through his hair. "Geez, that guy sure doesn't want to quit today, does he?"

"Yeah, he does have bad timing." She silently willed Ryan to finish what he was saying. "So...what were you trying to say?"

He was biting the edge of his lip now, the skin turning white around it. "Just that...uh, it was nothing. Just...nothing." He took a deep sigh, and Kylee's heart sighed right along with him. "You ready to head back? I'm sure my family is desperately missing us by now." He punctuated the last part with a wink.

"Sure," she said, wanting anything but to leave this moment with him, wanting to reverse time and force him to finish his thought. But instead, she turned and followed him over to the ledge.

The way back wasn't as bad. Walking toward solid land seemed a lot less daunting than walking toward a rock overhang. Even the hike back to the car was mostly downhill.

They spent the rest of the afternoon hanging out around the house. Ryan and his dad had several intense chess matches, while Kylee and his grandma put together a thousand-piece puzzle. Well, his grandma did most of it. Kylee struggled to make heads or tails of any of the pieces.

Instead, she spent most of the time trying to gauge Ryan's grandma. She still wasn't certain whether or not she had heard Kylee and Elena's conversation that morning.

Despite her best sleuthing, his grandma's poker face was still in place.

Becky came in from grocery shopping later that afternoon. "How was the hike, guys?" she asked as she put the milk in the fridge.

"It was good," Kylee said, going over to help. "Ryan had to basically drag me along most of the way, though. I clearly need more exercise."

"What are you talking about?" Ryan called from the dining room table, where the chess match was still going on. "I had to keep telling her to slow down. She was going too fast for my poor, weak legs."

Kylee rolled her eyes as she helped pull the remaining groceries out of the bags.

His mom just laughed. “Well, you guys should go on a hike together every day you’re here. We have plenty of trails around to get lost in.”

“But we’re here to spend time with you guys,” Ryan said. “We have all the time in the world to be with each other when we get home.”

His mom gave him a funny look. “Oh, a few hours away from us wouldn’t hurt. You and Kylee need your alone time.”

“Yes,” said his grandma, never looking up from her pile of puzzle pieces. “You two should get out more.”

Ryan looked over at Kylee with raised eyebrows. “I appreciate how concerned you all are about our relationship. You all should become marriage and family counselors.”

His mom ignored his quip. “You know where you guys should go? Star Peak.”

“Star Peak,” Ryan’s dad repeated. “We haven’t been there in ages ourselves. We should all go.” He took his turn on the chess board.

“You know, we really should have a penalty when you go over five minutes on your turn,” Ryan said as he moved his knight to take out another of his dad’s pawns.

“When you jump into things, boy, that’s when you get into trouble. Sometimes stopping and thinking about your next move gives you the best outcome." He then proceeded to put Ryan's king in check.

Ryan's mom collected the grocery bags. "Oh, we can go anytime, Rob. Plus, I think I have that thing going on tonight," she replied vaguely.

"What thing?" Ryan's dad asked, only half listening.

"Oh, you know, that event I've had scheduled for a while now," his mom answered as she put away the bags.

"I remember what you're talking about," Ryan's grandma said, fitting yet another correct piece into place. "And yes, it's tonight. Best let these two go alone."

"I still have no idea what you're talking about," his dad replied, his brow furrowed.

Ryan was occupied with his chess game, but Kylee was watching this conversation with confused interest. Why were Ryan's mom and grandma so adamant that they spend more time alone? They were clearly pushing the issue.

Ryan finally made his move and looked up. "Well, maybe Madison and one of her friends would like to come along. Regardless, it's a good idea. You interested, Kylee?"

"What's Star Peak?" she asked, walking back to the dining room table.

"It's a great place for seeing stars. I'm not actually sure what its formal name is. All the locals just call it Star Peak," Ryan answered, scratching his head.

"Sure," she said, hoping to look casual. She was feeling anything but that, though. More alone time with Ryan?

Under the clear night sky, looking at stars? She had to swallow the knot in her throat. "Sounds fun."

"And that's checkmate!" Ryan's dad boomed out.

Apparently, he'd known what he was talking about—stopping and thinking. Kylee wondered what else could happen in life if they gave it more time.

# Chapter 11

At dinner, they discussed visiting Star Peak again. Kylee found it almost comical how determined Ryan's mom and grandma were that they needed to go on their own. At the same time, though, she couldn't see their angle. If they had no doubts about the marriage, why would they be so worried that Ryan and her weren't spending enough time together? And if they did have doubts, wouldn't they be more worried about what was really going on between her and Ryan? Wouldn't they more likely be trying to get them apart?

Madison seemed interested in coming, but she was quickly dissuaded by her grandma.

"But you said you were going to watch that new Hallmark movie with me tonight," her grandma said as she served herself up some salad. They were eating the leftovers from the barbecue. There'd been enough food to feed two times the amount of people they'd had.

"I did?" Madison asked, lifting her brow.

"You must have forgotten. Happens to me all the time," her grandma replied.

Madison just shrugged. "Okay." She looked over at her mom. "You going to join us for a girls' movie night?"

"Your mom can't," Rob interjected. "She has a thing tonight. None of us are sure what that thing is, but she's adamant she has something." He took a giant bite of his hamburger, but he couldn't hide the smile in his eyes.

"I do have something!" his mom cried. "I'm going over to Judy's house tonight, and we're working on decorations for her daughter's baby shower next week." She sniffed and turned away from her husband. "Anyway, you two will just have to tell me how the movie ends. And you two," she added, looking at Ryan and Kylee, "are going to love the stars. I'm pretty sure it was a new moon a couple days ago, so it should be nice and dark."

Ryan leaned back and placed his arm around Kylee's chair. "Well, Pops, you interested in coming? Apparently, everyone else is busy."

"Well—"

"He can't," Ryan's grandma said, answering for her son. "He promised me he's going to finally fix my broken bedpost this evening. Something he's been promising for a month now." His grandma's tone made it clear this was not up for debate.

Rob folded his hands and grinned. "Looks like you two are on your own tonight."

The thought filled Kylee with a mixture of both excitement and dread.

*****

Ryan stowed a few extra blankets in his trunk. It wasn't supposed to be a super-cold night, but it never hurt to be prepared. He stood by the door, waiting for Kylee to grab her jacket out of their room.

He thought back to that afternoon by the waterfall. He couldn't believe what a fool he'd almost made of himself. What was he doing? Kylee was not in this for romantic reasons. *He* wasn't in this for romantic reasons. So, why did he keep feeling so drawn to her? He found himself wanting to hold her hand or be near her, regardless if anyone was around to see it.

And then, that morning, when she'd been in his arms, looking so flushed and irresistible, he hadn't been able to hold back. He was lucky that woodpecker had been there to interrupt before he'd ruined the whole situation. Who knew what Kylee would do if she thought he was developing real feelings for her? She'd probably hightail it and run.

He shook himself out of those thoughts. It was obviously just the situation. He wasn't truly developing feelings for her. They had been together nonstop the last week, so his emotions were all mixed up. That was all.

In the middle of his mental battle, Kylee came around the corner. She was bundled up in a puffy coat with a hat and a scarf, and an overwhelming feeling of happiness filled him.

"You ready to go?" he asked.

"Yep. Your mom also gave me a thermos of hot chocolate," she said, holding it up, "just in case."

"Mom knows best," he replied as he opened the door for her.

They took his sedan this time. Star Peak was popular enough that it had an actual paved road leading to it, so there was no need for the truck. They drove in a companionable silence, the radio on low.

The parking lot was deserted when they got there. Apparently, Star Peak wasn't a hot item on a Thursday night. As they both stepped out of the car, Kylee gasped when she looked up at the sky.

Ryan followed suit and looked up as well. It really was a spectacular sight. With Star Peak located on the edge of the valley, there were no trees to block the view. It didn't hurt that there was no moon, either. The sky was a blanket of bright specks.

"This is gorgeous," she breathed.

"It really is," Ryan said. He went to the trunk and pulled out the two lawn chairs and blankets he had packed. "Come on," he said, nodding to the right. "There's a grassy patch over here we can sit on."

Kylee trailed behind him, carrying the thermos of hot chocolate.

He set up the two lawn chairs side by side on the flat ground. With a flourish, he offered one to Kylee. "Your throne, my lady."

She snickered. "Why thank you, servant boy." After she sat, Ryan settled himself next to her.

He fluffed out one of the blankets and threw it over them. "And now, we observe."

They sat, staring into the dark night, the stars a glittering expanse.

"Have you ever brought another girl here before?" Kylee asked, her voice loud in the quiet night.

Ryan looked over, but her expression was hidden by the darkness. "A girl?"

"Yeah, you said I was the first one you had brought to the waterfall. How about this place?"

Ryan had actually shocked himself when he decided to bring her to his waterfall. For some reason, he'd felt compelled to show it to her. Almost as if by bringing her there she'd see a little more into him.

He tried to judge her tone. Was she hoping for more insight into his feelings, or just digging for a good story? "I actually did bring another girl here once," he finally answered, "but it was such a bad experience that I've tried to pretend it never happened."

Kylee snuggled deep into her chair. "Spill it."

He covered his eyes with his hand, not really wanting to relive this story but willing to oblige Kylee. "It was my senior prom. I had spent three months pining over this new girl, Emma, who had moved to our school. I finally got the courage to ask her to prom."

"I wish I could've seen seventeen-year-old Ryan lovesick over some girl," she said, her words muffled by the blanket she had cocooned herself in.

"I was pretty pathetic," Ryan said, thinking back to his younger self. "I had this whole evening planned. We would go to the dance, she'd realize how awesome I was, and then we'd come here afterwards and look at the stars, and she'd let me kiss her. It was going to be perfect."

Ryan sighed, and Kylee waited.

"The dance went fine, but I don't think she ever got to the point where she realized how awesome I was. She must have missed that part of the itinerary. Then, when we drove out here, I ended up getting a flat tire right at the turnoff. Some guys from school were here with their dates, and one of them offered to take Emma home while I waited for my dad to bring a spare tire. The drive home must have gone well for them, because by the following week, Emma and the guy were going out."

He thought he saw a hint of a smile creeping across Kylee's face through the darkness. She reached over and patted his shoulder. "I'm sorry. I can see it still affects you."

He blew out a dramatic puff of air. "Some things just scar you for life. Nothing like rejection from a high school crush."

She just laughed. "We can try and make a better memory for you tonight."

Ryan looked at her in surprise. What had she meant by that? It was too dark to see her eyes, but he'd felt her body stiffen after her comment. Maybe she hadn't meant that to sound as suggestive as it had.

He shifted in his seat. The night suddenly felt warm regardless of the cool temperature. Despite his earlier resolve to keep this evening light and friendly, he reached over and fiddled with her hand under the blanket.

"Kylee..." His voice trailed off, and she turned at the sound.

"Yes?" she finally asked, although her voice was barely above a whisper, almost as if she wasn't sure if she wanted to hear his answer.

He continued playing with her fingers, struggling to speak. He wasn't sure why he was doing this, but how could he hold this bombardment of feelings back? "I—I know this whole marriage isn't real. I know you agreed to it all just to help me out."

He saw her tilt her head down. "I don't—"

"Wait. Let me finish," Ryan said, needing to get this out. "Like I said, I know none of this is real, and we're just friends. And that's a friendship I don't want to lose or mess up. But do you ever think there could be more between us?"

He swore Kylee was holding her breath next to him.

"I'm not saying we have to stay married," he continued when she didn't speak. "We can still go through with the annulment and everything. But maybe we could try starting from the beginning and see what happens?"

Kylee was still silent next to him.

Her silence was all the answer he needed. He pulled his hand back, feeling a flush run up his neck. "You know—never mind. I don't even know why I brought this up. It's just because we've been thrown together so much this last week; my mind is so jumbled that I don't know—"

"No!" she exclaimed, reaching out and squeezing his hand tightly. "No, it's not just in your mind. I…" She tilted her head up to the sky. "I was thinking it was just me. I never thought you had similar feelings."

She paused, and the weightiness of her words hit him like a ton of bricks.

Slowly, his surroundings hazed out, and Kylee was the only thing he could focus on. The outline of her face turned toward him, the sound of her breathing shallow and quick. His stomach tightened, and he was sure his heart was about to beat out of his chest. The last shred of his previous resolutions fled from his mind as he leaned forward. A second later, their lips met, and Ryan was immediately hit with how much he'd wanted this again. How good kissing Kylee felt—in a way no other kiss had. She smelled like something floral, and her full lips were soft and warm. He didn't realize he'd even lifted his hand, but it was there, cupping her cheek and holding her close.

Ryan gulped a breath of air when they finally pulled back, an alarm ringing through his head. From what little he could see of Kylee, she looked as stunned as he felt.

They sat staring at each other for what felt like an hour but was probably only a few seconds. Ryan wished for the life of him that he could see her face better, read what she was thinking in those expressive eyes of hers. Was she upset about the kiss? Was she happy about it? More importantly, did it rock her heart as much as it had his?

"Looks like you had better luck this time," Kylee said quietly, her humor cutting through the stillness.

Ryan's face broke into a jittery grin. "I think you're right." The peace between them seemed too perfect to ruin with more talking. Instead, he tucked her arm under his, pulling her close. She laid her head on his shoulder and seemed just as content to sit with him. They spent the next little while snuggled close together, watching the stars.

Finally, Ryan broke the silence. "You think that hot chocolate is still hot?"

"Let's hope so," Kylee answered, reaching down to grab the thermos.

Ryan instantly regretted his comment when the warmth of her head left his shoulder.

The drink was no longer scalding but still warm. They shared it between them, making small talk about meaningless things. Kylee didn't comment about the kiss they'd shared, so neither did Ryan.

When the night began to grow cooler and the hot chocolate was gone, they decided to head back. They pulled in a little after ten, and the house was mostly dark. Ryan's mom had left the kitchen light on for them, but everyone must have gone to bed.

Kylee rinsed out the thermos while Ryan put the blankets he'd borrowed back in the closet. Then, they walked down the dark hallway together, Ryan using his phone to light the way.

"You can use the bathroom first," he said quietly as they entered their bedroom.

She was quick, coming back a few minutes later in her pair of flannel pajamas.

By the time he'd gotten back from his turn, she was already snuggled in bed. He stood by the door for a minute, his hand resting on the lightswitch.

"Kylee?" he said, hearing the hesitation in his own voice.

"What?" she asked, popping her head up over the covers.

"I know this marriage was a crazy thing for me to ask of you, but I'm glad you came. I'm glad we had this time together." He searched her face for a reaction.

Kylee smiled almost shyly. "I'm glad I came, too."

Every cell in Ryan's body was telling him to go over and kiss her again, but he didn't want to move too fast.

Instead, he quickly flipped the light off and uttered an overly cheery, "Well, goodnight!" before rushing to his bed on the floor. After a minute of shuffling around, they were finally both still.

As he lay there, staring into the dark, the same question kept running through his mind: *What now*?

# Chapter 12

Kylee spent the next morning catching up on some design work while Ryan was on the phone with his manufacturer. His bank had received the money, and he was working to get the transfer made.

When Ryan finally set his phone down, he turned to Kylee with a grin. "I think we did it."

They were in his dad's office in the left wing of the house. As such, they could talk in private.

"Yeah? No hang-ups?" Kylee asked, truly happy for him.

"I think so." Ryan fell silent as he glanced down at his phone, scrolling through a message.

Not wanting to lose his attention to another email, Kylee stood up. "Well then, we should celebrate."

Ryan looked over. "Yeah?"

"Yeah. C'mon. I'll treat you to lunch." She started to slide on the jacket she had hung on the back of her chair. "You'll have to drive, though. Sorry."

Ryan laughed. "The sacrifices I make for you, wife."

"I guess I'm not really treating you if you think about it that way. What's mine is yours and yours is mine," Kylee said with a smile as they started out the door.

"That's a saying I can get behind," was all Ryan answered with.

*****

Kylee felt a difference between them the rest of the day. Things seemed more relaxed and comfortable than they had been all week.

Even their demonstrations of affection in front of his family seemed more natural. Every time Ryan held her hand, Kylee didn't jump. And every time she leaned into him, he brought her in close like they'd been doing it their whole lives.

At dinner that night, Ryan's grandma seemed intent on questioning them about their future.

"So, where will you two live now that you're married?" she asked, folding her hands in her lap.

"Well, right now, we're just at my place since it's bigger. I don't think we really need to move any time soon." He looked over at Kylee with raised eyebrows.

Kylee shrugged, the weirdness of the situation leaving her unsure. On the one hand, this was a ridiculous question because she and Ryan weren't going to stay married and it didn't matter that they stayed in Ryan's condo for the next three weeks. But on the other hand, something *was* brewing between them. Who knew what their future held?

Luckily, Ryan took her shrug as an answer and continued eating.

"You can't just live at your bachelor pad," his grandma exclaimed, finally picking up her fork and digging into Becky's homemade lasagna. "You two need to find a place together. A home that's yours. Not just Ryan's old condo."

"Hey," Ryan said. "My condo is very nice. And Kylee is welcome to add any touches she wants." He grinned at Kylee. "I've already told her I trust any opinions she has as far as décor—as long as they don't include pink."

Kylee smiled, remembering that discussion. "Yes, I'm well aware of your dislike for pink and sparkles."

His grandma huffed across the table. Kylee decided to appease the woman. It was all pretend, anyway; she might as well make her happy.

"I don't know, Ryan. Maybe your grandma has a good thought. We can go look at places when we get home, just to see if there's anything we like." She squeezed his hand under the table. He hesitated for a split second before a splash of warmth filled his eyes. Was that real happiness, or just a show for his family?

He interlocked her fingers in his. "Okay. If you'd like to, I'm fine with that."

For a split second, Kylee forgot they were pretending as pleasure seeped through her.

"I think you'll be much happier in a new place," Grandma said, clearly satisfied with this outcome.

"I remember the apartment your mom and I first lived in together," Rob said as he forked a bite of lasagna. "It was a quaint little thing."

"Quaint!" Becky chimed in. "Apparently, you're forgetting how the roof leaked regardless if it was raining. Or the fact that it was infested with fleas from the previous renter's dog. Or how there wasn't a single floorboard in the place that didn't squeak."

He waved his hand, dismissing her comments. "Quaint is a state of mind. It was just you and me, on our first adventure together, making our first home out of nothing."

Ryan's mom smiled. "There is something about starting out together. A new place may be just what you two need." She cocked an eyebrow at them.

Kylee got the feeling she was trying to subliminally say something. Was she concerned about their commitment to each other?

Just then, the front door closed.

"Sorry I'm late," Ryan's sister shouted as she walked in. She set her bag on the counter and walked over to the table, inhaling dramatically. "Mmm, is that your lasagna, Mom?"

Becky pointed to the empty place setting next to their grandma. "Yes. Have a seat, hon, while it's still warm."

"Where were you?" Ryan asked in that typical big-brother tone.

Madison rolled her eyes. "I was out shopping. I lost track of time." She eyed Ryan's plate. "I see you forgot your healthy serving of salad tonight."

Ryan looked down at his plate, currently loaded with a hefty serving of lasagna and garlic bread, but—as his sister had pointed out—not a single leaf of lettuce. "I get my veggies from the tomato sauce."

Madison sighed as she grabbed a piece of bread. "Tomatoes are actually a fruit, Ryan."

He leaned back and groaned.

Kylee laughed at their banter. "We're working on balancing out Ryan's food pyramid. He seems to have forgotten the fruits-and-veggies section."

"He always has," Madison agreed, sending Kylee her first smile yet. "Really though, Ryan. Do you have any idea how beneficial a healthy dose of vegetables is to your body? I mean, the fiber content alone would change your digestion, not to mention the vitamins and—"

"Okay, okay, Miss Dietetics Major. Thank you for the lecture." Ryan picked up his piece of garlic bread. "Now, can I enjoy this in peace?"

Madison just sniffed before popping a tomato into her mouth.

"Did you get anything good?" Ryan's mom asked, reverting the conversation back to Madison's shopping trip.

"Not much. I was mostly just window shopping. What did I miss here?" She dug into her food.

"Oh, your mom and grandma are just trying to convince Kylee and Ryan to move somewhere new," his dad answered.

"Yeah," Ryan added. "I guess my spacious two-bedroom condo isn't good enough for us."

"It's not that it's not good enough," his grandma responded. "It's just that it's not both of yours. It has too much of *your* history in the place." She emphasized the point with her fork.

Madison's eyes narrowed. "I don't know if that's such a good idea."

Her mom turned in surprise. "Why not?"

Madison paused, her gaze shifting back and forth between Kylee and Ryan before finally landing on Kylee. "Well, no point in making big changes until you know for sure things are going to last. You'd hate to jump into something that you will regret in a few months." She finished this little speech by lifting her eyebrows at her brother.

"Madison!" her mom whisper-shouted. "Why would you say such a thing? Of course Ryan and Kylee are going to last. That's why they got *married*." She turned her apologetic look on Kylee. "Please excuse my daughter's rude comment."

Ryan's grip on Kylee's hand tightened during his sister's comments. At his mom's words, though, he relaxed. "Geez, Mads, you have a bad day or something?"

Madison just gave him a side look before returning to her food.

Kylee tried to take an emotional cue from Ryan's light comment, but she couldn't help feeling deflated. Madison basically hit the nail on the head with her accusation. Even with them both admitting there was a spark between them, was it any more than a light infatuation on Ryan's part? Was it even close to something lasting?

"So, I have a project starting over on the west side of town this next week..." Ryan's dad tactfully changed the subject and began telling them about some of the work he had going on.

Kylee pretended to act interested, but inside, she was having a mental battle. Something was up with Ryan's family. On the one side, his mom and his grandma seemed intent on solidifying their relationship. The last few days, they had been constantly encouraging Ryan and Kylee to spend time together and get away from the family.

On the other hand, there was Madison. She'd seemed anything but excited for her brother's recent marriage. If Kylee didn't know better, she'd have thought his sister had been doing her best to create doubts and suspicion about Kylee from the moment they'd met.

Kylee looked down at her hands, realizing she'd been cutting up her roll with a knife and fork. Trying to inconspicuously set her utensils down, she focused on the family's conversation.

She needed to have a talk with Ryan. And soon.

*****

Ryan's sister pulled him aside that evening. His mom had gotten out some old photo albums and was amusing Kylee with pictures of three-year-old him.

"Hey, Ryan, can you help me get a box down from my closet? I can't reach it," Madison asked.

"Sure," Ryan said, following her down the hallway.

Madison had been so weird at dinner. What was her deal with his and Kylee's marriage? Sure, he hadn't told anyone that they'd been dating. Obviously, he couldn't have because there had been no dating, but he didn't know why she was so opposed to it. He'd never discussed any of his relationships with her before.

When they got to her room, she pointed out a large box on the top shelf of her closet. Ryan reached up and grabbed it for her, although he noticed that she could've easily gotten it herself with a chair.

"Here you go," he said as he handed her the box.

"Actually, I wanted to talk to you," she said, setting the box on the ground.

"I assumed so. That box wasn't exactly difficult to reach," Ryan said as he sat on her bed. The springs squeaked at his weight. "What's up, sis? You seem out of sorts."

A worry line creased her face. “Are you going to tell me what’s going on between you and Kylee?” she asked bluntly.

Ryan froze, all the ease leaving his body and being replaced by tension. He had told his brother about the whole ordeal. But Madison was another story. His sister, his mom, and his grandma were three peas in a pod. If Madison found out what he’d done, there would be no hope in keeping it from his grandma or his mother.

“What do you mean, what’s going on between us?” he asked, feigning disinterest.

“There’s something weird about it all. I don’t trust her. How long have you even known her? Are you sure she’s in it for the right reasons?” she asked. Her frown lines deepened. “Does she know about the trust money?”

Her question surprised him, and he replied automatically. “Yeah, she does, but why would that matter? You don’t think Kylee would marry me to get to my trust fund?” He wished he could have taken back the words as soon as he had said them. He didn’t want to give Madison any more reason to connect his marriage with his trust fund.

“Are you sure?” she asked, sitting next to him on the bed.

Ryan pictured Kylee and almost burst out laughing at the ridiculousness of it. He didn’t laugh, but he did smile broadly. “Madison, you clearly don’t know Kylee if you think she’d do something like that.”

Technically, Kylee had actually done that very thing. But she hadn't done it to trick him. If anything, it was him marrying for money.

"Obviously, I don't know Kylee very well, but like I said, I can tell there is something weird going on. Everything between you two is a little awkward. You guys behave more like two people on a first date than two people who are married." She tilted her head at him and raised her eyebrows.

She probably had a point. It wasn't like Ryan and Kylee were professional actors or anything.

Madison was still reasoning this out. "From what I've gathered from her, her design freelancing isn't the most lucrative path. Knowing you're about to come into a big inheritance could be a strong motivation to fall *in love*." She used air quotes to emphasize the last two words.

"Madison," Ryan said on an exhale. "I appreciate your concern. I can tell it's coming from a loving sister. But you have to believe me when I say Kylee didn't marry me for money. She is not the gold digger you're thinking she is." He threw an arm around her shoulders. "And while yes, maybe we seem awkward sometimes, you have to remember we just got married. Our relationship took a whole new turn a week ago, and we're still getting used to it."

She nodded slightly but didn't seem convinced. "If you say so. But I'm still not sure if I trust her."

"Come on, sis. You worry too much."

*****

When Ryan and his sister walked back into the living room, Kylee could tell that something was off. She brushed it aside, though. Probably just her imagination; she was getting paranoid these days.

"So, how was the Hallmark movie you and Madison watched the other night?" Kylee asked Ryan's grandma. She was sitting next to Ryan's mom and grandma on the couch as they looked through photo albums.

"Very cute. You'd love it." His grandma's eyes brightened. "As a matter of fact, you and Ryan should watch it tonight. Madison recorded it."

Kylee shrugged. "Sure—if you can convince Ryan to watch a chick flick, that is." She grinned.

His grandma laughed. "Honey, a man will do anything for the woman he loves if she really wants him to."

At that, the imposter feeling came back in full force. Ryan didn't love her. He might have been slightly infatuated with her the last few days, but that wasn't the same deep love his family thought was between them. She nodded in response to his grandma's comment, though.

"Ryan, you're watching the Hallmark movie we watched the other night with Kylee this evening."

Kylee loved how his grandma didn't phrase it as a question. It was more of a command.

"Am I?" Ryan asked as he walked behind the couch. He leaned down over them. "I had plans to watch *Terminator III* with her tonight, actually."

"Don't worry. We changed them for you," was his grandma's response.

He laughed good-naturedly. "If that's what Kylee wants, I'm in." He lightly massaged Kylee's shoulders for a second.

Just then, his dad stepped in from the backyard. "Ryan, I need your help for a few minutes, loading some wood into the back of my truck."

"This is why I don't visit home more often," Ryan said to the ceiling as he rolled his eyes. "I immediately become a workhorse."

"Oh, stop your griping. You're getting soft with that desk job," his dad said as he walked out the door.

Ryan leaned down once again and spoke softly into Kylee's ear. "If I'm not back in fifteen minutes, come save me." Before he walked away, he added, "You're in charge of the popcorn."

Kylee smiled. A movie sounded perfect. But at the same time, she needed to talk to Ryan again. Things just didn't feel settled between them.

"I'm going to go put these pictures away," Ryan's mom said, standing.

"Thanks for showing them to me," Kylee said. "It's good to see what little Ryan used to look like."

"He was quite the cutie." His mom walked away with her stack of albums.

"Well, as good as the movie was, I'm probably not going to sit through it again," his grandma said, standing as well. "I've got a book by my bedside table calling my name." She looked over at Kylee. "You two enjoy yourselves, though."

And with that, she was off.

Only Madison and Kylee were left in the room. Kylee nervously stared at her hands. Something about Ryan's sister made her uncertain. It was clear she didn't like her, and Kylee just wasn't sure why.

After a moment, Madison stood and silently walked over to where Ryan's grandma had been sitting on the couch. She sat on the edge of the tan-colored cushion, staring intently at Kylee.

"I don't know what your angle is with my brother. I don't know if you're in it for the money, or if you're just messing with him, but there's something about your guys' relationship that is off. And I think you're the reason for it." She leaned slightly back and folded her arms.

Her threatening tone sent chills through Kylee. Before she could respond, though, Madison continued.

"All I have to say is, you're not only going to break Ryan's heart when you decide you're through with him, but you're also going to break the hearts of this family. My parents have been waiting for Ryan to find the perfect girl for years, and while they were surprised by your marriage, I can't tell you how excited they were." She finally broke her intense gaze by shaking her head. "So I hope your reasons or intents are worth it to you. That they're worth the heartache you're going to cause."

She stood up abruptly. "My suggestion is that you leave now, before you get us all in too deep. No amount of money is worth an entire family's happiness." She let those words hang in the air as she walked away.

Kylee sat, stunned into silence. Madison couldn't have known about Kylee and Ryan's deal, could she have? No, she would've made some comment about Ryan knowing that the marriage was fake. Madison seemed to imply that she thought Ryan was a victim, too. Was she worried about the trust fund money? Did she think Kylee was planning to eventually divorce Ryan and get a cut of it?

Regardless of whatever Madison's assumptions were, the one thing she'd said that pierced Kylee's heart was what this would do to Ryan's family. In their minds, Ryan had found his happily-ever-after. He'd found the girl he was going to have children with and grow old with. When they found out that Kylee and Ryan were ending things, they would be heartbroken like Madison had said.

Kylee didn't want to be responsible for that. She hadn't known Ryan's family for long, but they were some of the kindest, most welcoming people she'd ever met. They had opened their hearts and their home to her and never once questioned her marriage to their son. They never once faulted her for having missed their son's big day.

She didn't know if she could deal with breaking their hearts like that. Maybe she should do what Madison said. Maybe she should leave now and minimize the damage already done.

She was so lost in her thoughts that she didn't even notice when Ryan walked back in.

He stepped in front of her with his hands on his hips. "You had one job to do," he said with a frown, but humor danced in his eyes.

"Oh," Kylee said, jumping up. "The popcorn. I forgot."

He waved her off. "I'm kidding. I'll get it."

She sank back into the couch, trying not to let her emotions show on her face. Would leaving now really do any good, though? For some reason, the thought of facing his family again, even for one more day, was almost unbearable. Madison's accusations had narrowed Kylee's view. All she could think about was the disappointment Ryan's family would have. The distrust. The thought made her sick.

"Normal or extra butter?" Ryan called out from the kitchen.

"Uh, whatever you want," Kylee replied loudly. Her voice sounded a little hoarse, even to her own ears. Whatever she decided to do, she couldn't let Ryan know. If she did leave now, he would try to stop her. But he was too close to the situation. He couldn't see the damage their fake relationship was going to bring onto his family.

The trust money had already gone through. The manufacturer would start work on Monday. She wouldn't officially annul the marriage until the month was up, but there was no reason to play this farce at his parents' any longer.

Ryan came back a few minutes later with an overflowing bowl of popcorn.

"How many bags did you pop?" Kylee asked as she eyed the bowl.

"Two. I was contemplating doing three, but I figured I'd start small," Ryan answered, throwing some into his mouth.

"I think you have your sizing off."

He smiled and grabbed the remote. "It's possible." Leaning back into the couch, he put his arm around her, pulling her close.

Despite the turmoil in her head, being that close to Ryan felt good. Maybe just for the night, she'd forget about all her problems and live in the moment. She snuggled into him. He was warm and comforting, and she didn't want to ever leave. She'd have to soon enough, but now wasn't the time. She'd worry about all that tomorrow.

"You ready for an overly sappy love story?" Ryan asked, looking down at her.

"You bet."

# Chapter 13

Ryan rolled onto his back early Sunday morning. He reached his arms overhead and stretched, feeling the soreness in his neck and shoulders from sleeping on the floor for the fourth night in a row. At least tonight he'd be back to sleeping in a bed, even if it was just an air mattress. Anything was better than the ground, at this point.

He would do it all over again, though, if it meant spending the weekend with Kylee. He thought about how things had changed over the last four days. Although, if he was being honest with himself, he was pretty sure his feelings for Kylee had been festering for a while now. He'd just been too blind to admit it.

But that was in the past. They were making a new start, and he was ready for it.

He sat up slowly, not wanting to wake her. He knew she preferred sleeping in compared to his early-bird self. He had done his best to be quiet each morning.

After piling his blankets into the corner, Ryan began creeping out of the room. As he reached the door, he glanced over at the mound on the bed, then noticed something funny.

There was no mound.

Had Kylee woken up before him? That was strange.

He peered at the nightstand and saw a piece of paper. Walking over for a closer look, he found his name scribbled on the outside of it. Dread filled him as his fingers flipped the note open.

*Dear Ryan,*

*If you're reading this, I've probably already left.*

*I can't do it anymore. I can't keep pretending. It's not fair to your family or to you. I can't keep talking with your mom about when I think we're going to have kids. Or telling your grandma how dreamy our dating history was. I can't keep pretending I just want a friendship with you when I know I want more.*

*I know you said your feelings have been changing the last few days, but let's be honest, we both know it's just because of this scenario. We've been thrown together the last week, so of course, emotions are running high.*

*Anyway, I'm sorry again, but I had to leave. I hope you don't mind that I took your car. I'll leave it at your place when I get home. I know you said Mason is coming back today, so I assumed you could drive home with him.*

*I want you to know I truly care for you, probably a little too much.*

*Wish you the best,*
*Kylee*

Frozen, Ryan stared at the note. She'd left? She'd left without even talking to him? What had happened?

He thought over the last twenty-four hours, wondering if he'd missed some sort of sign. She had seemed totally normal the night before. Even while they'd been watching the movie, she'd made no indication that something was wrong. Had she?

He left the room, not even thinking to grab a jacket to fight off the morning chill. Quickly, he dashed out the front door, needing to check the driveway to see if she'd really left.

Yep. His car was gone.

He slumped on the front sidewalk, surprised by the despair he felt. She was leaving him? Like, for good? Would he get back to an empty house?

It wasn't like they'd been together long—barely over a week. But somehow, he'd gotten used to Kylee. He'd gotten used to her companionship. The last week, they'd spent the bulk of every day with each other. Now she was just gone?

He tucked his freezing hands under his armpits. What was he complaining about? This was what he had wanted.

This was the arrangement he had hoped for: a quick, no-strings-attached business transaction. He should have been happy. The money transfer had already gone through. What more did he want from her?

What more *did* he want from her?

Sighing out loud, he gazed back at the house. The worst part would be explaining it to his family. What would he say? What would his story be?

He couldn't say they'd broken up yet. Maybe he'd say she had a work emergency or something. It wasn't the best excuse, but he could deal with his family.

The question was, could he deal with not having Kylee?

*****

Kylee drove like she was being chased the first half hour. She didn't know why. Ryan probably wasn't even awake yet, but the adrenaline pumped through her all the same.

It wasn't until a good thirty miles into the drive that she let up on the gas and slowed to the speed limit. By the time she pulled into Ryan's condo, she felt calm and collected. She had made the right choice. Ryan would be disappointed at first, and maybe even mad, but in the end, he'd agree with her. The charade needed to end—for everyone's sake.

She rushed to pack up the remainder of her stuff. Considering she had taken most of it with her to his parents' house, it didn't take much effort. Within fifteen minutes, she was ready to go home. To her home, not Ryan's.

She had texted Elena before she left Ryan's condo, knowing her roommate wouldn't be awake yet. But when she finally stepped through the front door of her apartment, Elena was on the couch, waiting for her.

Neither one of them said anything at first. Kylee just dropped her bags, and Elena embraced her in a tight hug.

"You were right," Kylee sobbed, her words muffled by Elena's oversized sweatshirt.

"Shh, shh," Elena said, pulling back so they could see each other. "You'll be okay, hon. Everything will be okay. You just need to have a good cry and some Oreos."

Kylee let out a laugh that mixed with her tears. "I'm not sure if you're right this time."

*****

Ryan went through his day feeling like his head was in the clouds. He did his best to avoid his family and their questioning looks most of the morning. Mason showed up around lunchtime, and Ryan gave him the same spiel he'd told the rest of his family: Kylee had needed to go back early for a work emergency.

Mason raised his eyebrows but said nothing.

Ryan knew Mason wasn't buying the story, but Ryan was glad for his silence.

They agreed to leave after dinner since neither of them had anything urgent to get back for. Ryan especially wasn't looking forward to the empty house that would greet him.

Early afternoon, he found himself staring listlessly out the family room window when his grandma's voice interrupted his thoughts.

"Ryan, how about you and I go on a little walk." She said it in her typical commanding tone.

"Sure, Grandma. Let me get you a jacket. It's a little chilly out there."

She nodded. "Thank you. My pink one is lying across the chair in my room."

Ryan hurried to grab it. When he returned, he helped her into the wool coat.

They made their way to the trail at the back of his parents' home. Ryan despairingly thought about the last time he'd walked this trail, when he'd been hand in hand with Kylee. What he wouldn't have given to go back to that moment.

He and his grandma walked the first few minutes in silence. It was clear she had something on her mind, but he'd let her lead the conversation.

"Are you going to tell me what's really going on between you and Kylee?" she asked, never taking her gaze from the trail in front of them. He'd adapted his pace to his grandma's leisurely one, so they hadn't gotten too far.

"What do you mean? Kylee had to get back home for work." He shoved his hands into his pockets as he walked.

His grandma came to a full stop then, her piercing eyes meeting his. "Just because my body is old doesn't mean my mind has slowed down, young man. I'm well aware that your marriage to Kylee is not a real one."

Her blunt statement brought Ryan to a standstill as well. "Wha—what are you...What do you mean, not a real one?"

"I mean, I know you and Kylee didn't marry because you desperately love each other and couldn't wait another day, as you told everyone." She raised her eyebrows at him and waited.

Ryan cleared his throat, trying to clear his thoughts at the same time. "What makes you think that? Kylee and I do care for each other...lots..." His trailing words sounded ridiculous to his own ears.

"Ryan, you can stop acting with me." She began walking again, and Ryan stutter-stepped to join her. "I heard Kylee talking on the phone to her friend a few days ago. She made it very clear that you guys were only married to help your business." She gave Ryan a stern look.

Oh no. Ryan's knees went weak. Kylee had called her roommate Elena? And his grandma had overheard? He wanted to crawl into a hole. But he couldn't; he needed to make his grandma understand what had happened.

"Grandma, it's not like that. I promise, I don't just want your money." He was silent for a moment. How could he have made her see that he wasn't just being some greedy grandchild looking for an inheritance? It must have certainly looked that way. He blew out a breath of air.

"Okay, maybe I did need the money, but I promise it was for a good reason." He ran his fingers through his hair as he tried to order his thoughts.

"Well then, you'd better start explaining yourself," she answered, giving him a sharp glance.

Ryan spent the next few minutes explaining his business troubles to his grandma. He told her about the production mistake and how he'd needed funding to get new Hudson Packs made before his orders all got canceled. How he'd approached Kylee—his good friend but not girlfriend—about marrying him for a short while. He admitted how she had been reluctant at first, feeling a surprising need to protect her from any of the blame or censure. He even left out the part about paying her school loans, since it didn't matter anyway. He was sure his grandma would be calling her lawyer, Frank, as soon as they got back.

His grandma was, meanwhile, listening to everything in silence, her face unreadable. When he was done with his monologue, she asked in a low tone, "Why didn't you just come to me and ask for help, Ryan? I would've loaned you the funds, had I known. Grandpa didn't just leave *you kids* with money. He made sure I was set up for a very comfortable life."

"I know," Ryan said, his reply sounding more like a moan. "I just didn't want to have to ask family this time. You all know about my previous failure. I just couldn't deal with the embarrassment of telling you all I had messed up a second time." The thought that maybe he shouldn't have gone through with the fake wedding raced through his mind. Would it have been better if he'd simply asked his grandma for help? The last week with Kylee ran through his mind, the times—both good and bad—that they'd shared together.

No. He was glad he had done it this way. It might have been a whole lot more heartache, but Ryan had realized something paramount: his feelings for Kylee.

His grandma continued talking. "Ryan, do you know how many times your grandfather failed before he succeeded? I'd never fault you for trying. As a matter of fact, I hope you fail a few times. That's how you learn. Never feel embarrassed by reaching for the stars." She gently patted his hand. "But it sounds like you got that all worked out now. If I've been told correctly, you got your trust fund transferred over to you this weekend."

Ryan nodded.

"Very good. Then we can move on from this boring topic. What I really want to discuss is you and Kylee."

Ryan swallowed hard. "Wait, that's it?"

"What's it?"

He narrowed his eyes at her. "Aren't you going to refute the money transfer? Tell everyone that I lied about it all?" He'd had worse punishments for stealing cookies from her kitchen as a kid.

One corner of her mouth lifted. "Ryan, you're an adult now. I'm not going to hover and reprimand you for every dumb decision you make. Plus, I'm pretty sure you've already beaten yourself up about this enough. You don't need my help." She pursed her lips, and Ryan swore she was trying to hold back a smile. "Plus, just between you and me, I always thought that marriage requirement was a little silly for your trust funds. But you know your grandpa—old-fashioned to a T, he was!"

Ryan's laugh came out as a gush of air. An unseen weight lifted from his shoulders. Not so much because he'd been afraid of losing the money, but because he'd been afraid of disappointing his grandma beyond repair.

"Anyway, as I was saying, let's talk about more important things. You and Kylee."

The weight slowly returned. He'd have rather talked about the trust fund than him and Kylee.

"I think you need to stick with it," his grandma informed him.

"Stick with it?" He was shocked.

"Yes, well, with Kylee, I mean. You two are a good thing. Don't mess this one up."

He wasn't following her reasoning. "Grandma, you already know our marriage is a fake. We were just acting the whole time. Kylee doesn't really love me." Then, as an afterthought, he added, "And I obviously don't love her, either."

His grandma snorted.

Furrowing his brow, he blurted, "I don't!" and threw his hands out to his sides.

Tsking, she said, “Ryan, you forget that I’m your grandma. I’ve known you your whole life. I don’t think I’ve ever seen someone repressing their feelings as hard as you have this week.”

“Repressing my feelings?”

“I can’t tell you how many times I wanted to shout at you, ‘Kiss her already!’ You were mooning all over her every time she wasn't looking at you or paying attention to you. I’m surprised she hasn’t figured out how head over heels you are for her herself.”

Ryan’s cheeks reddened.

“Ryan,” his grandma said after a pause, “I’ve lived a long life, and there are some things you learn with experience. When you find someone who lights you up, you hang on to them for dear life. I don’t know what happened between you two, or why she ran off this morning—”

“She had a work thing,” he protested.

His grandma gave him a blank stare. “Please give me a good scenario where a logo designer would have to leave unexpectedly at four in the morning.”

When Ryan didn’t respond, she continued.

“Ultimately, this is about your happiness. Despite what you might think, all I want is for you to be happy. And I’m not saying I know what’s right for you,” she said, the corners of her mouth coming up, “but I know what’s right for you. Kylee is what’s right for you. You’d better go after her.”

Ryan rubbed his temple with one hand. "What if she doesn't really love me? What if it's just a fleeting infatuation that started because of this whole situation?" He thought back to her note, wondering if her accusation about his feelings not being real were really just a reflection of her own.

"I may not be Kylee's grandma, but I can tell when a woman is in love with a man. I wouldn't be too concerned about that—as long as you don't do anything dumb and blow it." She emphasized this last part with her finger.

Ryan smiled, not 100% convinced, but feeling better than he had all morning. "How do I do it? I'm not even sure what I did wrong."

His grandma shrugged. "It may not have been anything you did. Who knows? Don't focus on the past; focus on what you're going to do from here on out."

Silence stretched between them, the only sound the crunch of their footsteps on the dry leaves.

"Have you ever considered becoming a therapist?" Ryan finally asked.

His grandma chuckled. "No one could afford this level of expertise. You're lucky I'm giving you the family discount."

He laughed out loud. "Well, please just don't tell Mom or Dad anything. I don't need them knowing about this."

His grandma glanced at him for a second. "Ryan, your mother knows about this."

"You told her?" he exclaimed.

"She's your mother. Of course she suspected that something was up. She was the one who came to *me* and asked if I knew what was really going on between you two."

Ryan hung his head and sighed.

"Why do you think we've been trying so hard to get you two alone as much as possible? You guys are perfect for each other. You both just need to see the light."

"And here I was thinking I was the sneaky one. Meanwhile, you two are over there trying to play Cupid!" he said with a grin. They had turned back at some point without him even noticing it. His parents' backyard was only another hundred yards up the trail. He slung an arm around his grandma's shoulders, pulling her in lightly. "Thanks for this, Grandma. I'm not sure if things will work out how you're hoping, but I'm going to try."

His grandma grabbed his hand. "Ryan, just be honest with her. She has feelings for you—I know it. Just give them the opportunity to come out."

He squeezed her arm, thankful that they'd had this talk. Now, if only he could talk as openly with Kylee about his feelings.

*****

Mason's first question when he got in the car with Ryan that evening was, "All right. Spill it. What did you do to Kylee?"

"Nothing!" Ryan protested. "Really, I have no idea why she left."

"No idea?" Mason's doubt was evident.

"I mean, I have some suspicions." He paused, but when Mason didn't interrupt, he continued. "She left me a note."

"A note?" his brother asked, glancing at Ryan before he pulled onto the main street. "What was in it?"

Ryan shrugged. "I don't know. Some stuff about how she didn't like lying to the family. And something about caring too much. It was pretty vague."

"So, what are you gonna do about it?"

"That's the question," Ryan told him on an exhale. He wished he had a better answer. "I don't want to lose her. As ridiculous as it sounds, I think it took me marrying her to realize how much I care for her. I think, before, I was just taking her and our friendship for granted. Now, I'm afraid I've lost her for good."

Mason drummed his fingers on the steering wheel. "You could get her flowers."

Ryan rolled his eyes. "Dude, flowers aren't going to cut it. I need to do something big."

"Well, what does she like? Or what are some of your best memories together? Where was your first date?"

Ryan stared at him blankly. "We never had a first date—at least, not officially. And we hung out all the time, but they were just casual things."

"Dude, you've never taken her on a date?" Mason asked, his eyes wide.

"No." He narrowed his eyes at his brother. "Why are you so surprised? You knew our marriage was fake."

"Yeah, but you've known Kylee for three years. You totally have a thing for her and always have. I just assumed it was one of those dating-on-and-off-again kind of relationships. I didn't realize you'd never even slightly pursued her."

Mason was shaking his head, and Ryan felt like he was talking to his grandma all over again. "No. We've never been a thing or had a thing. Well, other than the whole marrying-each-other thing."

"Sheesh. Well, talk about doing things backwards," Mason said, clearly trying to hold in a laugh. "Obviously, we know your first step, then."

"What's that?" Ryan asked.

"You need to take Kylee out on a first date."

# Chapter 14

Kylee stared down at her ringing phone, nerves flying around in her belly.

It was Ryan.

She had known this moment would come. She had known that, at some point, they would need to talk again. They had things that needed to be resolved—namely, their fake marriage. But she couldn't bring herself to hit the answer button. Instead, she hit the bright-red "Send to voicemail" option instead.

With that done, she set the phone facedown on her comforter.

It was Monday morning, and she was working from her bedroom, propped up in her bed with endless pillows and her laptop on her legs. She had just finished sending out invoices for the projects she'd worked on that month—a chore that she hated but was essential.

A few seconds later, her phone buzzed again, this time with a text from him.

***Hi Kylee, just seeing how you are doing. Looks like you got everything from my place. I haven't seen any forgotten socks or anything else that would give me a reason to call you.***

The corners of her mouth lifted as she read this, but her heart ached. His attempt at humor wasn't very good, but at least he had tried. Her mind raced. Did he need or want a reason to call? What should she respond with: "Yes, I have all my socks"?

She chewed her lip when a new text flashed across the screen.

***Also, I wanted to know if you're free on Friday night to go out on a date with me?***

Kylee stared at the screen, not believing what she was reading. Ryan was asking her out on a date? Why? What was he trying to do? She had given him a clear and easy break at his parents' house. No strings attached. Nothing. Why was he trying to ruin that?

She wished Elena was home so she could ask her opinion. Should she accept? She would be making her heart vulnerable all over again if she did.

Almost of their own accord, her fingers started typing.

***Sure. We probably have some things to talk over. Want me to meet you somewhere?***

It made sense when she thought of it that way. Ryan was probably just trying to make sure they had complete closure and everything was okay between them. That was all. It took a few minutes before he responded, but when he did, it was simple.

***No, I'll come pick you up. How's Friday at 5:30?***

She frowned at his reply. Why was he insisting on picking her up? She wanted to keep this simple and short.

***You sure? You don't need to come all the way over here to pick me up.***

***It's no big deal.***

She couldn't see any way of denying him, though, without seeming rude.

***OK, 5:30 works for me.***

***Great, come hungry and wear something casual.***

It wasn't until she read the text three times over that she realized her hands were shaking slightly. She set the phone down and took a deep breath. She needed to get a hold of herself.

This was a closure evening. Something to bridge the awkwardness of the last few days.

Now, if only she could convince her heart of that.

*****

Ryan couldn't remember the last time he'd been so nervous for a first date. The funniest part was this was technically a first date with his wife.

Realistically, they'd been out lots of times. He couldn't count the number of lunches they'd had together over the years, let alone the last week and a half of being in each other's company all day, every day.

But for some reason, putting the label "first date" on the evening gave him all the jitters.

His brow furrowed as he got out of his car. He was confused why Kylee had seemed reluctant to see this as a date—at least, according to the responses she gave his texts. He'd have to make her understand that he was here to see what their future could be, not talk about what had happened in the past.

He reached her apartment door, his clammy hands grasping the simple bouquet of daisies. He thought about getting her something more dramatic, but daisies seemed better for a first date.

A few seconds after knocking, he heard shuffling noises from the other side. When Kylee appeared, he needed a second to catch his breath and take her in.

She was beautiful. There was really no other way to put it.

Her dark hair had been pulled back into a loose ponytail. Fitted jeans hugged every inch of her legs in contrast to her loose sweater. She looked taller, for some reason, and he realized she was wearing a pair of high-heeled boots.

"Hey," was all he could say, his voice low and borderline hoarse.

She stared at him as well, finally responding with a, "Hey," herself.

Ryan held back the urge to wrap her up in a hug. It was amazing what a few days of separation had done to him. He couldn't remember the last time he was so happy to see someone.

"You look great," he finally said. "I've missed you." He hadn't meant to say that last part, but it'd slipped out before he could think better of it.

A tinge of pink colored her cheeks, and she smiled. "Thanks. It's good to see you, too." She looked down at the flowers in his hands. "You didn't need to bring me those."

He smiled and held them up to her. "Of course I did. It's our first date."

She raised her eyebrows, and Ryan wasn't sure if that was a good thing or a bad thing. She did realize this was their official first date, right?

"I guess it is. Come in. Let me put these in some water."

He stepped into her apartment where her roommate was sitting on the couch, watching them. He'd met Elena once or twice, so he waved at her.

She smiled and wiggled her fingers back at him. "I want her home by ten p.m. No funny business, mister," she said loud enough for Kylee to hear.

"Elena!" came a shout from the kitchen.

Ryan and Elena both laughed as Kylee came in with a red face.

"We'd better go before my roommate gives out any more of her sage advice," she said, striding past him to the door.

"Don't worry. I'll take good care of my wife," Ryan said with a wink as he followed Kylee.

*****

Those words—"my wife"—hit her like a ton of bricks. She was going on a first date with her husband. How ridiculous could they get?

She was just about to turn around and tell him exactly that when Ryan touched her elbow. His warm grip made her lose her train of thought.

"So, I hope you're ready for this," Ryan said.

Kylee cocked her eyebrow. "What exactly do I need to be ready for?"

"The *perfect* first date." A smile was hinting at the corners of his mouth.

She wanted to be in on the joke, though. "Yeah?"

"First, we're going to go to the farmer's market," he said.

She thought about his words, wondering why they had sounded so familiar. Her mind was too frazzled with all the emotions running through it, though, to give them much thought. "Okay, that sounds like fun."

He looked at her as if he were waiting for her to say something more before dropping his gaze. The little grin never left his face, though.

Ryan opened the door of his sedan, and she got in, remembering the last time she had been in his car. She'd been running from him and his family. An embarrassed warmth spread through her when she thought about her actions. Had she acted too rashly? She questioned herself for the hundredth time.

Ryan got in on the driver's side and started up the car. As he drove, a borderline awkward silence fell between them.

"So, has production on the bags finally started?" Kylee asked.

"Yes, it has." Ryan's enthusiasm was almost visible. "They should be finished by the end of next week and shipped out. I'm barely holding myself back from flying out there and making sure the process goes smoothly this time."

Kylee smiled. "Are you still using the graphics I designed for you a few months ago?" She'd been the one to come up with the media kit. This was before his whole fiasco with the backpack material.

"Of course. Who else could come up with a better design than you?" He had a teasing note to his voice, but she appreciated the compliment all the same.

They chatted for a few more minutes, mostly about his bags and the next few steps for them. Before she knew it, they had reached the farmer's market and parked.

Something was nagging at the back of her mind as she got out, but she couldn't pinpoint what. Ryan didn't seem to have any hesitation, though, so she shrugged the feeling off and walked through the entrance with him.

It'd been a while since she'd been to this market. She loved the vibe there, though. There were so many beautiful colors and handmade items. Everything from fresh fruits and vegetables to delicate arts and crafts. Kylee was amazed by the talents people had.

They checked out all the booths, trying samples here and there. When the pathway divided, Ryan seemed adamant that they had to go right.

"This way looks better," he said, purposefully turning her in that direction.

Kylee couldn't care one way or another, so she just shrugged and followed him.

Two minutes later, he stopped at a tent where a woman was selling various hair pieces and scarves. He looked at Kylee from the corner of his eye. "These are kind of pretty. Do you like any of them?" he asked, running his fingers through a rack of scarves.

As she watched him, her mind seemed to clear, and everything clicked.

This was their first date.

The one they had made up in the car ride to his parents' house.

A wave of something she didn't know how to describe overcame her, and she had to blink rapidly to fight the tears pooling in her eyes. He'd made their fake story come to life. And that touched her in a way she hadn't expected.

When she didn't answer him, Ryan turned and looked at her. Clearly noticing her distress, his eyes widened. "Kylee, what's wrong? Are you okay?" He pulled her to the side, away from the crowd.

She nodded, still not able to talk. When she regained her composure, her voice was low. "This is our first date."

He nodded, looking confused. "Yes, this is our first date."

She shook her head. "No, this is *our* first date," she said with more emphasis. "The first date we made up."

His concern smoothed into a grin. "Yes! I was wondering when you'd figure that out. I wanted to make our fake life a reality."

She covered her eyes as a wave of emotion hit her again. This couldn't be happening; it was all too perfect. Ryan was being too perfect. What guy would think to actually create their story?

He pulled her hands from her eyes and wrapped an arm around her. "C'mon, Kylee. You have a scarf to pick out."

She smiled wide and followed him back to the booth. There, they flipped through the rack of scarfs, playfully testing each one out on each other. In the end, she picked a turquoise one with a gold thread running through it. As Ryan paid for it, she tied it loosely around her neck.

"Now, we need to find the world's greatest ice cream." He took her hand as they walked away from the scarf booth. "I researched our options before coming here, and according to popular opinion, either Meg's Creamery or The Waffle Bowl could be our winner."

"Hmm..." Kylee twirled her new scarf. "I guess we'll have to try both—in the name of market research, of course."

"My thoughts exactly."

Meg's turned out to be closer, so they stopped there first.

"I think their mint n' chip could use some work," Kylee said fifteen minutes later, licking her spoon, "but that brownie batter might be a contestant for the best chocolate ice cream I've ever had."

Ryan nodded. "I concur. The mint needed more chocolate chunks to take it over the top. It was just sub-par."

She tossed her plastic spoon and cup into the trash can. "Are you ready for The Waffle Bowl?"

"Lead the way," he said, flourishing an arm out for her to go in front of him.

The crowd had increased to the point that they no longer could walk side by side. So Ryan jokingly looped a finger through one of her belt loops from behind.

"Just to make sure I don't get lost!" he called over her shoulder.

Kylee rolled her eyes and laughed. When they reached The Waffle Bowl, there was already a long line.

"I don't know if this means anything, but there's a significantly larger crowd in front of this place than the other," she said to him as they got in line.

"I'm taking it as a good sign," Ryan responded. "Plus, it'll give me a few minutes to make space for more ice cream." He did a little shimmy dance, which caused her to snort with laughter.

"You're a weakling. I could probably eat at least double that much," she said.

He just smiled.

When a woman walked past them, Ryan stepped behind Kylee to make space for her. Then he remained there, putting his hands on her shoulders and massaging them lightly. Kylee loved how comfortable he was around her. She just wished she could get out of her head and relax like him.

"So, what flavors should we try here?" Ryan asked, leaning low to talk into her ear.

Her nerves flared up again. She blurted out the first flavor to pop into her head. "Uh...I don't know. How about cookie dough?"

"Good choice. How about that peanut butter crunch too?"

"Perfect." She shifted her weight to one leg so Ryan was more to her side than directly behind her. The simple night she'd imagined of getting closure was clearly not on Ryan's agenda. And she wasn't sure if it thrilled or scared her.

Fifteen minutes later, they were sitting at a little round table a few yards off, two overflowing bowls of ice cream in front of them.

"We aren't very professional researchers," Kylee said around a mouthful of peanut butter ice cream. "To truly compare quality, we should have gotten the same flavors at each place and tried them at the same time."

"We needed a control group too," Ryan added. "Who knows how my opinion is going to be affected by my surroundings. I'm a little fuller now, so The Waffle Bowl is already at a disadvantage."

"Yes, but these chairs are cushioned as opposed to the bench at Meg's, so you're probably more comfortable eating here."

"True..." He swayed his head from side to side. "Although, the temperature has dropped slightly, so I'm a little colder. Ice cream never tastes as good when you're cold."

"Ah, so many issues. So what's your final, flawed, opinion?" Kylee asked, using her spoon to hide her grin.

"The Waffle Bowl. Hands down."

"I have to agree." She wiggled her eyebrows. "It's quite possibly *the best* ice cream I've ever had."

"Oh yeah?" he asked. "Sounds like this has been the perfect first date so far."

She tried to bite back a smile. "Possibly."

They window-shopped a few more vendors on their way back to the car. Kylee ended up purchasing a few jars of jam, and one vendor almost convinced Ryan to buy a hand-carved knife.

“That guy almost had you back there,” she said as she watched Ryan pull his keys out of his pocket.

“Did you see that knife? It was awesome!” He clicked the unlock button and opened her door.

“Yes, it was beautifully carved. But can you please explain when you’re ever going to need a five-inch-blade pocket knife?”

“Maybe one day I’ll need to cut up an apple and I won’t be in my kitchen.” He made a sweeping motion, pretending to pull something out of his pocket. “Bang, there is my knife, so handy and reliable.”

“You’re right. I shouldn’t have talked you out of buying it. Think of all the apples you could be cutting right now.” It took her some serious effort to say all of that with a straight face.

“I feel like you’re mocking me,” he said, covering his chest with his hand.

“Never.” She plopped into her seat.

He got in next to her. “So, the only thing left to do tonight is to find some super-good pizza. Do you have any favorites?”

“There’s always the place on the corner near the library. I can’t think of what it’s called, but it sells pizza by the slice.”

“Oh yeah. I know where you’re talking about. Done.” He started the car and headed in that direction.

They talked about recent movies that had come out and had a good debate about music again. Kylee noticed that

Ryan seemed to be carefully avoiding the topic of her walking out on him last week.

She was secretly waiting for him to bring it up. It seemed like, at any second, he would want to discuss it and her actions. But he never did.

As he drove her back home, there was silence between them for the first time in nearly three hours. Not necessarily an awkward silence—more of a reflective one.

When they walked up to her doorstep, Kylee waited for Ryan to set the tone. It was almost like they'd gotten back to their old relationship. The kind they'd had before they'd gotten married. But now, it felt like a friendship with something more. A deeper, more intimate connection pulsed through them.

"Well," Ryan said, running a hand through his hair when they reached her door. "This was really fun." He paused, clearly waiting for Kylee's input.

"It was," she said, flicking her scarf out for show. "It was like a storybook first date."

Ryan laughed. "Someone did a good job planning it." He stalled for a second, suddenly serious. "So, if it's okay, I'd like to take you out again."

She hadn't been expecting him to ask for another date. Not that she hadn't had a good time; she just assumed this was more of a night to finish things on a good note between them. Apparently, she'd been wrong.

She fiddled with the keys she'd pulled out of her bag. "Yes, I'd like that." She looked up at him and noticed the breath he swallowed. Was he nervous?

He exhaled slowly. "How about I take you to lunch next week? Tuesday?"

"Yeah, I have my shift at the library, so it'll have to be an early lunch, but that works for me." She couldn't hold back the burst of happiness that spread across her face. If she wasn't mistaken, Ryan seemed just as pleased.

He took a slight step forward, narrowing the gap between them, when her neighbor's door opened and slammed against the wall. "I told you, dude! I'm coming!"

One of the three college-age boys who lived there dashed out of his place, talking on the phone. There was another bang when he slammed the door shut. As he jogged past them, Ryan stepped back, and Kylee slid her key into the lock.

"Well, I guess I'll see you next Tuesday," Ryan said, shoving his hands into his pockets when they were alone again.

"Yeah, sounds good." Kylee turned the knob, and the door opened a few inches at the pressure. She didn't necessarily want the night to end, but unfortunately, she didn't know what else to say.

Ryan rocked back on his heels for a second before clearing his throat loudly. As if making a sudden decision, he quickly stepped toward her.

Not expecting the gesture, she stumbled slightly over her doormat, accidentally giving him a hip check on the way.

Ryan, in turn, stutter-stepped backwards, just managing to catch himself before falling. With a deep flush running up his cheeks, he straightened. Whatever his intentions had been, he clearly gave them up now. "Um, well, good night," he said, giving her an awkward side hug.

She half-heartedly returned the hug, miserably kicking herself.

Ryan stepped back. With a loud "Good night!" he turned on his heel and headed back to his car.

"Good night," Kylee responded softly as she watched him leave.

She stepped inside her apartment, slowly closing the door on his retreating form. What exactly was going on between them? What was going on in Ryan's head?

The feelings she'd worked so hard to suppress the last two weeks were bubbling to the surface with a new vengeance. She fingered the new scarf still tied around her neck. What was she going to do?

# Chapter 15

Ryan couldn't stop grinning on Tuesday. Sure, he'd managed to shrink his new favorite shirt in the dryer that morning, and his car had been making a weird clicking noise the last couple of days, but none of that could have put a damper on his happiness about seeing Kylee again.

Their last date couldn't have gone better, in his opinion. Well, besides that whole door scene. He'd really botched that one up. He should have just gone in for the kiss he'd been planning on. That ridiculous half-hug had done nothing for him. That was okay; he was in no rush.

He was working at home that morning when he got a call from Madison. He was surprised. Not that they didn't often talk, it was just that he knew she'd been peeved at him when he'd left last weekend. She still wasn't convinced of Kylee's intentions.

"Hello?" Ryan said as he picked up the phone.

"So, have you resolved things with the Mrs.?"

Ryan sighed and tapped his pen on his desk.

"Things are going okay between us, thank you for asking. How is school life? Still proving kale is the new superfood?"

"First off, there's no such thing as a superfood. A balanced diet is the key. But I didn't call you to talk about that." She took a deep breath, her exhale loud and sharp into the phone. "I called to apologize for questioning you about Kylee."

Well, that hadn't been what Ryan was expecting. He hadn't asked Kylee about the reasons she left his parents, but he wouldn't be surprised if Madison had something to do with it. He didn't know if she'd actually confronted Kylee, but he wouldn't put it past her. "Well…"

"I talked to Grandma yesterday, and she told me everything," Madison continued on. "All about your failing business, and how you needed to marry Kylee for the trust money, and how you went behind everyone's back the whole weekend..."

"Wow, you sure know how to make a guy feel good," was his blunt reply.

She snorted. "Alright, maybe I'm digging a little. But I'm sorry for getting involved. Clearly, I didn't know the whole picture. I was just concerned that my brother was going to get his heart broken."

Madison had never been one to admit defeat easily, so he knew this apology had been hard for her. He couldn't help the slight feeling of bitterness, though. Had Madison been the catalyst that pushed Kylee out? "Just tell me this, did you ever talk to Kylee?"

"What do you mean 'talk to Kylee'?" she asked, way too much innocence in her voice. "I talked to her all weekend."

"You know exactly what I'm talking about." Ryan gritted his teeth. "Did you mention something to her about your suspicions of her being a fraud, or a gold digger, or whatever it was you thought?"

There was silence for a second before Madison said, "I may have made a comment about my doubts concerning your marriage."

"Ughhh, Mads!" The thought that his own sister had pushed Kylee out dug at him. He leaned back in his chair, his hand over his eyes. No matter how frustrated he was at his sister's actions, he knew he couldn't really blame her. He had been the one to create the whole situation. Kylee's hesitations had probably been there from the start. Madison's comments just brought her to actually take action on them.

"You still there?" a very subdued voice asked.

"Yeah," he responded, knowing he had to make things right with his little sister. "Even though it increased the difficulty of my situation about tenfold," he said, unable to resist a little digging. "I appreciate that you have my back. And you're right, I probably have been a little selfish and underhanded with this whole thing."

"I know. Like I said, I'm sorry for getting involved." There was silence on her end for a second. "So, really, how are things between you and Kylee? Grandma said things were a little rocky."

Ryan leaned back in his chair. "I don't know. We went out last weekend, and things were pretty good. I'm seeing her again today, so we'll see."

"So she's back at her place?"

"Yeah, we figured there's no reason to keep up the facade now that everything is in the open."

"Have you told her how you feel?"

"She knows how I feel. It's obvious."

"Are you sure? If I know anything, it's that you never assume anything when it comes to a woman's feelings."

"When did you become such an expert?"

"Well, I'm a woman. Therefore, I know how women think."

Ryan laughed, but he was secretly avoiding her question. He'd never told Kylee how he felt—at least, not outright. He had hinted at it, tried to show it as much as possible, but he'd never said it. To be honest, the thought scared him of what she would respond with.

"I'm just saying…Kylee is never going to accept that you love her until you say it out loud."

His heart sped up at the word love. "Love! Who said anything about love?"

There was silence for a second on the other end before his sister said, "Ryan, why would you go through so much trouble for a girl if you didn't love her?"

Madison's words pierced Ryan like a nail. Was his sister right? Did he love Kylee? He'd had feelings for other girls in his past. Girls he'd been infatuated with. But he couldn't think of anyone he'd had feelings for like Kylee. When he thought about the possibility of never being with her again, he felt sick. Was that love?

"Look, I'm not telling you what to do, but if it were me, I'd be open with her. You're already on treacherous ground. You don't want to lose her a second time."

"Okay, I'll think about it," was Ryan's reply.

"Oh, also, when you finally figure out what's going on between you and Kylee, could you please call Mom? She and Grandma have been speculating up a storm since you left."

Ryan started laughing. "Those two should've been romance authors."

They said goodbye after a few more minutes of chatting.

Madison's words didn't leave Ryan's mind, though. Maybe she was right. Maybe Ryan just needed to lay it all out on the table.

The question was, would he rather lose his pride, or possibly Kylee?

*****

Kylee had been battling mixed emotions since her date with Ryan on Friday. Half the time, she'd felt like she was on cloud nine. Everything was wonderful, and she and Ryan were going to get married and live happily ever after.

Then, reality came back, and she remembered that she already *was* married to him. And that there was no way any of this could be real. They'd been friends for over three years, and he'd never once pursued her romantically. He was just getting swayed by the situation.

Kylee was working from home Tuesday morning. She wanted to have time to get ready for her lunch date. When she left her room to get some water mid-morning, she found Elena was sitting on the couch, a pack of Oreos on her chest, while she typed on a laptop.

"You know those things are going to kill you someday," Kylee said as she flopped down next to her.

"At least I'll die happy," Elena replied, offering the package to Kylee.

Kylee laughed and pulled one out. "I guess you're right."

Elena closed her laptop and looked at Kylee. "So, tell me about this lunch date."

"It's nothing. I'm just meeting Ryan for lunch."

"Annnnd?" Elena drew the word out.

"And...what?"

"And...how are you feeling about it? How are you feeling about him? You've been so closed off since Friday. I'm pretty sure I've given you enough time to process your feelings, so you can confess them all to me now." Elena had one eyebrow cocked.

"I don't know, Elena! One moment, we're holding hands and everything seems perfect. The next, I feel like we're just back to being friends, hanging out." She leaned back into the couch and shoved the entire Oreo into her mouth. "Wha shoo I doo?"

"Well, first, you shouldn't talk with your mouth full," Elena said. "I think you need to decide what you want out of this, *amiga*." She gave Kylee a stern look. "You keep throwing this on him. Whatever he wants, you'll go along with. You need to stop being the damsel in distress and take control of your life. Do you like Ryan? Do you want to have a future with him?"

Kylee nodded, still chewing.

"Then you need to do something about it. You need to straight up tell him how you feel."

"I know. I want to, and I need to." She fiddled with the edge of her shirt. "I don't know, Elena. I'm just afraid. I'm afraid that he'll say he doesn't feel the same way. And I'm also afraid that if he says he feels the same way, his feelings aren't real. That he's going to decide a few months from now that he made a mistake."

Elena wrinkled her nose. "What do you mean his feelings aren't real?"

"I don't know… I mean, we've been friends for three years, and he's never *once* acted interested in me. I'm afraid that being in this weird situation, spending so much time together and having this fake marriage, is influencing his feelings. They're not real—they're just a result of our circumstances."

"Kylee, how do you think anybody develops feelings for another person? It's always the result of the circumstances they're placed in. Whether it's because they ended up sitting next to each other in a class, or they became coworkers or neighbors. The fact that your situation is more unique doesn't make it any different. Have you ever thought that maybe Ryan has had these feelings for a while and just never realized it until you were forced together like this?"

Kylee looked at her with wide eyes. "No, I never thought about it like that. You think it's possible?"

Elena lifted one hand. "I don't see why not. Most importantly, though, Ryan is a grown man!" She snapped her fingers adamantly. "He's in control of his own feelings. That's not something you need to worry about or stress over, *hermana*. If he says he likes you and he's falling for you, then you should trust that he knows himself."

"I know. I'm just overanalyzing everything, aren't I?"

Elena put her arm around Kylee and gave her a tight squeeze. "It's okay. It's what women do best."

Kylee laughed and covered her face with her hands. "I don't know, Elena. The thought of telling him how I feel seems so scary."

"We'll leave it up to fate, then." Elena lifted an Oreo toward Kylee with a grin. "This method has never failed me yet."

Kylee looked hesitantly at the chocolate cookie facing her. This was the culprit that had gotten her into this whole mess. Did she dare take the risk again?

When she really thought about it, though, she wouldn't take the last two weeks back. They had been some of the hardest, but also some of the best days of her life. She reached for the other half of the cookie.

"If you get the cream," her roommate said, "you have to tell him how you feel. If you don't, then you can wait for him to make the first move."

"Deal."

They slowly began to twist the cookie. As Kylee pulled away with her half, she saw that the bulk of the cream came with her.

"Dang it," was her response over Elena's laughing.

*****

This was it—no more playing games. As his brother had said, he needed to be blunt and upfront with Kylee.

He was going to do it today.

To make sure they had a quiet space to talk at lunch today, he'd picked up takeout to eat at the park. He found a quiet park bench. The situation was perfect.

When his phone buzzed, he looked down at it to see a text from Kylee.

***Where are you?***

He looked around him, not seeing her anywhere.

***I'm in the center of the park, right next to the little gazebo. I'm wearing a dark-green jacket and gray pants.***

***Are you trying to blend in with nature?***

He smiled at her quick response.

***I should have worn a red shirt and carried a rose.***

***Obviously. Okay, I'll be there in a minute.***

He shifted the bag of Chinese food to his other hand and continued glancing around him. A smile broke out when he saw her.

She was walking toward him, her effortless stride so familiar. It was amazing how good she could make a pair of jeans and a basic V-neck top look. Her hair fell about her shoulders in loose waves, perfectly framing her smiling face.

"You found me," he said, standing.

She pretended to eye his clothing as she got close. "Well, like I said, you could've worn something that stood out a little bit more. From far away, I mistook you for another tree."

He laughed and grabbed her hand in what he hoped was a carefree way. "Come on. I have a bench over here we can eat at."

They sat, the metal slats not the most comfortable seating, but Ryan barely noticed.

He pulled out the food as he talked. "So, I grabbed fried rice, some beef and broccoli, and of course, orange chicken because it's a staple." He searched through the bottom of the paper bag for the plastic forks and napkins. "And of course some very authentic fortune cookies for dessert," he finished, offering her a utensil.

"You're the best. Thanks."

While they ate, they kept up a light chatter about the day and what was new. Ryan had a hard time focusing, though.

In the back of his mind, he knew he wanted to have a relationship talk with her, and it kept consuming his thoughts. But instead of just bringing it up, he kept pushing it aside, like a serving of vegetables on a dinner plate. When he finally glanced at his watch, he realized they only had a few more minutes before Kylee had her shift at the library. He had to speak up now.

"So, I actually wanted to talk to you about something." His gaze darted over to hers then back down. He couldn't look at her or he'd lose his nerve. "I wanted to talk to you about us."

He saw Kylee freeze out of the corner of his eye, but he wasn't sure whether to take that as a good sign or a bad one.

"I feel like there are feelings going on between us that neither one has spoken about. You know, feelings of more than just friendship. Things we probably need to clarify." He was dancing around the subject. He just needed to get to his point.

Before he could, though, Kylee spoke up.

"Yes, I've been thinking the same thing lately." She put down the container of chicken she'd been holding.

Ryan was a little surprised by this.

Kylee bit her lip, the food in her lap forgotten. "I have something I need to say." She fell silent again before letting out a big sigh and muttering something under her breath. Ryan could've sworn she said something about Oreos, but he must have heard wrong.

"So," she finally began. "It seems like we're both developing feelings for each other. I'm not sure to what level yours are," she said, motioning toward him, "but mine are becoming pretty strong." She rubbed her hands up and down her pants. "I'd actually be lying if I said these feelings had just started to develop. I think I've liked you for a while now, and I just haven't wanted to admit it."

He wanted to ask her to clarify. What did she mean by a while? As in, since their marriage, or before then? She was still talking, though, so he tried to focus on what she was saying.

"But I don't want this to just be a passing fling. I know we've kind of been thrown together the last couple weeks because of circumstances. I don't want that to be our reason for being together." She looked at him in the eye, a somber tone to her words. "I don't want you to look back three months from now and question your decision or feelings. I'm not here to play games. If I make a commitment of love to someone, I want it to be for real and forever, not just until we get tired of each other."

Wait—did she just say love? The thought that Kylee might love him shocked him to his core. Unfortunately, it shocked him so much that he sat staring at her in silence for probably longer than necessary.

With slightly flushed cheeks, Kylee glanced at her watch. “I think I need to run,” she told Ryan, sliding the food off her lap as she stood. “My shift at the library begins in five minutes.”

“Whoa, wait. I wanted—what I mean is...” Ryan knew he was stuttering. He was just trying to gain his bearings on the conversation he had planned on initiating.

Kylee waved him off, already half turning to leave. “No, honestly, this is good. I want you to really think about this. Really think about what your true feelings are, now that you know mine. Leaving the whole fake marriage and everything behind, what do you really want?”

Without waiting for a reply, she shouldered her bag and was off.

Ryan watched her go wordlessly. What was wrong with him? Why did he turn into a muttering idiot whenever Kylee and his feelings were involved? He frustratingly began stacking the empty food containers, his mind racing.

Despite not being able to give the speech he’d planned, hearing Kylee's thoughts had been quite eye opening. She was mostly concerned about *his* commitment, about his feelings being circumstantial or lasting.

He gave a bitter grin to the pigeons eating the crumbs they’d left on their bench. If she could see into his heart, she’d know there was no way these feelings were temporary. If anything, he was just beginning to understand how strong his feelings really were for her.

And the fact that hers were already so deeply rooted for him gave him the confidence he needed to show her exactly how serious he was. He reached for his phone and began searching for her roommate, Elena's, number.

# Chapter 16

"Kylee, Kylee!"

Kylee felt herself mentally yanked out of a deep sleep. "Mmmm, what?" She tried to focus her eyes in the bright light. Wait, what was that light? It was shining directly in her face.

As her brain scrambled to understand her surroundings, Elena spoke to her again.

"Kylee, you need to get up."

Elena was standing in front of her, and the bright light was coming from Elena's cell phone.

Kylee glanced over at the clock on her side table. "Someone had better be dying for you to wake me up at five forty-five," she groaned, rubbing her eyes.

"No, I'm just paying you back for that morning you woke me up to do your makeup," Elena said as she dug through Kylee's drawers.

"What are you doing over there?" Kylee sat up but didn't move from her bed.

"I'm trying—uff—to find you something—to wear!" Elena randomly pulled things from the drawer.

"Why don't you just ask me what you're looking for, and I'll tell you where it is," Kylee croaked. "And why do I need something to wear? I'm not going anywhere." She rolled back over, concluding that Elena had lost her wits.

"*Amiga*, you need to get up. You're going on a date with Ryan."

This comment had Kylee almost springing out of bed. "What?!" Her croak had turned into a squawk.

"I said you have a date with Ryan right now. Get up. I'm looking for your black leggings and that zip-up hoodie you always wear to work out in." When Elena located the leggings, she held them up like a prize. "Aha! Found them. You know you should consider organizing your drawers a little better. I tend to put my heavier items like jeans in the lower drawers and my lighter items—"

"Elena, I don't care how you organize your drawers right now! What date are you talking about?"

Elena stopped her searching and faced Kylee. "Ryan called yesterday and asked if I could make sure you were awake and ready to go on a date by six this morning." She held her hands up. "Which, as I hope you know, is a huge sacrifice for me to be awake and alert this early, so you owe me big. But I have no details other than that you're supposed to wear something comfortable you can be active in." Elena wiggled her eyebrows at Kylee. "Quite the request, if you ask me."

Kylee threw a pillow at her. "That's it? He didn't tell you anything else? Like why it had to be at six in the morning? Or why he didn't tell me about it?"

"Nope. Now, where is that jacket I was asking about?" Elena went back to her rummaging.

Kylee reluctantly got out of bed, still feeling like she was in a dream. "Here, I'll get it," she said, walking over to her closet. Two minutes later, she was dressed in black leggings, a tank top, and her windbreaker on top.

"I assume running shoes would be most appropriate," Elena said, combing Kylee's hair into a high ponytail. Then, she let out a dramatic sigh. "It's a pity we don't have time for full makeup. Some simple mascara and a light blush will have to do. We'll do your brows, of course, but—"

"I'm not putting on makeup! If Ryan wants to see me at 6 a.m., he's going to get the real me." Kylee folded her arms defiantly.

"Yeah, girl power—you show him," Elena agreed, stepping in front of Kylee. Then she pursed her lips. "But maybe just a little under-eye concealer to hide those—"

"Elena!" Kylee cried.

Five minutes later, Kylee was finishing lacing her shoes when there was a sharp knock on the front door.

"He's here," Elena whispered in a dramatic voice. "I wish I could see this, but I clearly didn't have time to make myself presentable." She did an arm flourish toward her sweatpants and oversized T-shirt. "So I will be hiding in my room until you guys leave."

Kylee pulled her into a tight hug. "Thanks, Elena. You're the best friend I could ever ask for."

"Of course. You know I'd do anything for you."

Seconds later, Kylee was alone in the hallway. She went to open the front door, still not sure if Ryan was really going to be on the other side.

But he was, grinning like a kid on Christmas morning.

"Good morning, sunshine," he said. He was dressed similarly to her: running shoes, a pair of shorts, and a thick jacket.

"You'd better have a really good reason for waking me up this early," Kylee replied, trying not to show the happiness she felt at seeing him.

Ryan just reached forward and grabbed her hand, tugging her outside. "What better reason do you need than to spend time with me?"

She snickered as he pulled her along, still curious, but realizing she would probably get nowhere with her questioning.

As they made their way to his car, she noticed something attached to his trunk.

"Are those bikes?" she asked, her brow furrowing.

"Yep." He didn't explain further, just walked around to his side of the car after opening her door.

The inside of his car smelled like something sweet, but Kylee couldn't pinpoint what. When Ryan got in, he turned around and snagged something from the back seat.

"I knew you'd be grumpy," he said, the crackling of the paper bag catching Kylee's attention. "So I made sure to pick up some rations." He flipped on the light over their heads and took two huge muffins out of the bag. "I have chocolate chip and blueberry—your choice."

"You clearly know the way to my heart," Kylee said. "I'll take blueberry."

"I'll have you know, I spent a solid five minutes trying to remember if you preferred blueberry or cranberry. I distinctly remember you once telling me you hated one of them and loved the other."

"Wow, good memory. Yes, I love blueberry and hate cranberry muffins." Kylee tried to hide her surprise with a bite of muffin.

He turned the key and then grinned as he looked behind him to back up. "I amaze myself with my thoughtfulness, sometimes."

Kylee just rolled her eyes, her smile betraying her thoughts, though.

Ryan started driving, and Kylee soon noticed they were headed toward the mountains. With her interest thoroughly piqued, she asked, "Are you going to tell me where we're going? Or is this a kidnapping?"

He took a bite of the chocolate chip muffin. "If I were kidnapping you, I wouldn't have told Elena about it. We're going for a bike ride."

"In the mountains? In the dark? I'm more of a sidewalk or paved street kind of bike rider."

Ryan patted her knee. "Don't worry. This is an easy trail, no booters or step downs to worry about."

"Considering I have no idea what either of those two things mean, that doesn't make me feel much better."

Ryan let out his hearty laugh. "Don't you trust me yet? This is a totally flat, easy ride. I don't even think the trail is longer than about two miles." He turned, looking happy and excited despite the early morning. "I'll always take care of you. Don't worry."

Kylee couldn't help loving the way that last phrase sounded. Would he always take care of her? Her thoughts drifted to their conversation from yesterday. Should she bring it up with him? Had he thought about what she'd said? Did he have any sort of response?

The questions flitted through her head one after another. She decided to let them rest for now. Ryan clearly had something planned. Maybe she would get more clarity after their bike ride.

Twenty minutes later, they pulled off the two lane road and into an empty parking lot. It was finally light enough that Kylee could see her hand in front of her face, but the sun still hadn't come up.

"You wait in here a minute while I pull the bikes off the rack," Ryan said as he unbuckled his seat belt.

Kylee had no problem with that. It wasn't freezing outside, but she had no desire to leave the warm car if she didn't need to.

She watched Ryan lean one of the bikes against a tree before going to retrieve the other. When he was done, he motioned for her to get out.

"All right," he said. "I borrowed the second bike from a friend. Come here and we'll adjust the seat to your height."

Once she was comfortable on the bike, he went back to the car.

Now that she was fully awake, little butterflies of excitement fluttered in her stomach. What was Ryan's angle on this date?

Ryan came back with two helmets. "This is the smaller of the two." He set the helmet on her head, but it bumped into the high ponytail Elena had put her hair in.

"Here, wait a second," Kylee said, reaching up to untie the hair band. She undid the loop until it fell down loose around her shoulders.

As she was reaching up to re-do the ponytail, she noticed Ryan watching her every move. The intense look he gave her made her cheeks flush. She quickly pulled her hair back into a low ponytail and took the helmet out of his hands.

"Let's see if this fits," she said, trying to defuse the tension in the air. After she tightened the straps, the helmet fit perfectly.

When she was done, and Ryan was satisfied it fit, he put on his own and locked the car. "Are you ready?" he asked, grabbing the second bike.

Kylee nodded, not really sure if she was, but knowing she wanted to see what this led to.

Ryan began walking his bike along the parking lot to what appeared to be the trail head. Kylee followed closely behind.

When they got to the opening, Ryan looked back at her. "I'm assuming you want me to go first?" he asked. "Or would you rather me follow behind you?"

Kylee shook her head. "No, I have no idea what I'm doing. You go first."

"All right, let's do this." Ryan hopped onto his bike and began pedaling slowly, looking behind at Kylee.

She followed suit, mounting her bike a little less gracefully than he had. It had been a couple of years since she'd last been on a bike. The first few rotations were a little shaky before she got in the groove. Kylee actually found herself enjoying it after a minute, though.

Ryan kept an eye on her, calling back every few minutes, asking if she was okay. She responded with smiles and the occasional thumbs-up.

It was still mostly dark. However, a faint light illuminated the trees around her. The stillness of the air was calming, and she could almost see why some people would get up this early on a regular basis. Almost.

Fifteen minutes into their ride, Ryan skidded to a slow stop. Kylee did the same.

"We're going to park the bikes here. The last little part will be easier to just walk." He dismounted and unbuckled his helmet.

She got off her bike as well, and he stepped forward to take it from her. She fingered her hair as she removed the helmet, trying to smooth it out.

He watched her fuss for a minute with a slight smile. He eventually pulled her hands away from her hair. "You look beautiful," he said softly. "You always do." He stood there for a second, her hands in his, feeling like he held her heart as well. A second later, though, he turned to clip the helmets onto the bikes, giving her a moment to compose her emotions.

Once the bikes were situated, he returned and confidently took her hand. "Come on. It's this way."

She enjoyed the feeling of his skin against hers as he guided her down the path.

"Where exactly are we headed?" Kylee asked, as she eyed the narrow trail.

Just then, it opened up to a giant rock ledge. In front of them was one of the most gorgeous views of the valley she'd ever seen. The mountains surrounding it were masked in this light, hazy fog, the dark peaks standing out dramatically. The valley below was a pit of shadows.

"Look at that skyline!" she breathed.

Ryan stood beside her, taking in the view as well. Then, he glanced down at his watch. "Perfect timing," he said softly, almost to himself.

"What?" she asked.

"Hm? Oh, nothing," he replied. After shoving his hands into his pockets, he shifted his weight back and forth from each foot.

"It looks like the sun is coming up soon," she said. "This is a little pathetic, but I can't remember the last time I woke up just to see the sunrise."

He shot her a strained grin. "Yeah, me too, actually."

She narrowed her eyes at him, trying to decide what was wrong. "Are you okay?" she finally asked.

"Ye-yeah, I'm totally good. Just enjoying the view." He motioned toward the mountains with his hands, but not before checking his watch again.

*He sure is acting weird*, Kylee thought to herself.

Just as she decided to ignore his weirdness and enjoy the scenery, he took her hand and turned her so she was facing him. Butterflies erupted in her belly when she took in the seriousness of his gaze.

"Kylee, I wanted to finish the conversation we started yesterday."

The butterflies started a migration from her stomach to her throat. "Okay, um...what do you want to talk about?" She'd been dying the last twenty-four hours to hear his response to her words, but now that the moment was here, she wasn't sure she could handle it.

"You told me what your thoughts and feelings were, but I never got to share mine."

Ryan's eyes searched her face, and Kylee felt extremely vulnerable. A slight wind picked up, the chill causing her nose to burn and probably turn red.

"Kylee," Ryan said, causing her to snap back to the present. "Yesterday, you told me you were developing feelings for me. Strong feelings. But that you were worried about mine. About whether I had any for you, and if I did, were they just circumstantial." He took her other hand in his.

"I want you to know that I have strong feelings for you, too. And they weren't caused by or developed from this last week of pretending to be married to you. I think they've been growing for a long time now, and I've just been too blind to realize it."

He leaned back for a second, his gaze falling to the ground. Kylee almost unconsciously leaned forward, willing him to continue on.

Ryan took a deep breath and lifted his eyes. "Kylee, I love you. Truly, really love you. When I saw your empty bed at my parents' house and the note you left, I can't—I can't even describe the feeling that went through me. It felt like I'd lost a part of me. Please don't ever do that to me again."

His words struck her core. Kylee wanted to shout back that she loved him, too. That she never actually wanted to leave him. But she was too numb from shock and couldn't seem to get her mouth moving.

Ryan was watching her reaction. After a moment of no response, he began fumbling in the pocket of his jacket. Kylee studied his hand, trying to figure out what he was grabbing. Without showing her, he looked out toward the view, almost as if he was waiting for something.

"C'mon..." he said quietly, and Kylee turned to see who or what he was talking to.

The view was still there, as magnificent as ever, but things were lighter now. She couldn't see the sun yet, but the evidence of its rising was everywhere.

A second later, though, she saw it: the thin sliver of fiery red inching up over the mountain peak.

"Yes!" Ryan murmured, clearly seeing what he had been looking for. He turned back to Kylee, still grasping her left hand tightly. "I was supposed to do that last part during a sunset, but at least this one will be done correctly."

Kylee narrowed her eyes. What was he talking about sunrises and sunsets for—

Suddenly, Ryan lowered himself to one knee, and all of Kylee's musings stopped. Was he? He wasn't...

He was recreating their life for her again. Just like when he'd re-enacted their first date. He was re-enacting the first time they said I love you, and now…now, he was doing their proposal?

"Kylee, I can't think of a more backwards way for two people to fall in love, but here we are. You are one of the most radiant, beautiful women I've ever met. You're kind and loving to everyone. You're terrible at puzzles and really need to work on your hiking abilities, but I love you, even still."

He was grinning at this point, something she could barely see through the tears in her eyes.

"When I think of my future," he continued, "I can't see one without you in it. I won't see one without you. Kylee, would you make me the happiest man ever"—he slowly lifted the blue ring box, the diamond solitaire inside sparkling up at her—"and stay married to me forever?"

Kylee wasn't sure if she had pulled him up or if he had stood on his own, but a second later, they were locked in a kiss that said everything words couldn't. He kissed her softly at first, but she didn't want tameness now, not after all this time. She pulled him closer, and in turn, he wrapped his arms around her, lifting her until she was on her tiptoes. She was surrounded by him, his smell, his warmth, all of him. She never wanted to leave. And this time, she knew she would never have to.

When they finally pulled apart, Ryan jokingly collapsed onto the ground, slowly pulling Kylee down with him. "This has been the most nerve-racking two hours of my life," he said, snuggling Kylee into his lap.

Kylee just grinned back at him. "I bet. Think if you'd bought me a cranberry muffin instead of a blueberry." She leaned into his shoulder before pulling back and studying his face seriously. “Are you sure about this, Ryan? Like, really sure?”

“Kylee Hudson, I can’t think of something I’ve ever been more sure about in my life,” he said as he lowered his face toward hers again.

# Epilogue

"Are you ready for this?" Ryan asked, glancing over at Kylee in the passenger seat.

She exhaled slowly, a mixture of dread and anticipation filling her. "As ready as I'll ever be."

"Okay, while I'm grabbing the bags, here's one last song to pump you up." Ryan messed with his phone for a second. Before stepping out, he turned the car speakers up to almost full volume.

Kylee waited in silence, listening for the first notes of Ryan's song choice.

When the first few chords of Led Zeppelin's "Stairway to Heaven" started up, she let out a loud groan. "This is not a pump-up song!" she exclaimed, getting out of the car. "This is like the never-ending ballad that will put you to sleep."

"What? How dare you speak that way about such quality!" Ryan grinned broadly.

He brought over a massive backpack with a tightly rolled sleeping bag attached to the top. The brand *Hudson's Bags* was clearly etched into the fabric.

Ryan loudly sang the lyrics as he fit the pack to Kylee's back. Kylee grunted when the full twenty-five-pound pack rested on her shoulders. Then, she turned to face Ryan with her hands over her ears.

"I agreed to a honeymoon backpacking trip. I did not agree to spending four days listening to you singing Led Zeppelin off-key." Despite her harsh words, she had a smile on her face.

"But you love me so much you'd do anything for me. Like listen to my melodic singing…"—he came closer as he spoke—"wake up at five a.m. to see the sunrise…"

"I'm still not happy about that," she cut in.

"Or spend four days sleeping on the hard ground in a tent." He paused, millimeters from her lips. "All because of how much you love me."

She smiled right before closing the tiny gap. "I'm going to decorate our living room with pink, sparkly pillows when we get home."

THE END

# *Thank you!*

Thank you so much for reading! I hope you loved it—if you did please leave me a review (they are seriously THE BEST to us authors!), then come follow me on Instagram (@summers_pen) to hear about future releases and real, everyday life!

Want a free book? Sign up for my newsletter and get your free office romance, Her Plus One here!: www.summerdowell.com

# Also by Summer Dowell

If It's Perfect: The Wedding Business Series
It's Just Business: The Wedding Business Series
On Schedule: The Wedding Business Series

The Elle Project: The Holiday Romances

A Temporary Boyfriend: The Fake Love Series
A Temporary Engagement: The Fake Love Series

Love From Scratch
A Run at Love

# About The Author

Meet Summer. Your best-reading-buddy-that-you've-never-actually-met who's obsessed with writing romance books. You know, that friend that always has a sarcastic comeback & whose favorite thing is to sit next to you on the couch, not talking, reading our own books? That's Summer.

She's a stay home mom to 6 and has a slight need to escape the laundry and diaper chaos. Summer turned her ability to see the humor in anything into a lineup of books that now inspire readers to chuckle, snicker, and even lol at the embarrassing situations she puts characters in.

Her superpower? Besides writing book dedications that purposely call out her husband, she is really good at giving people an escape from their everyday lives in the form of a story.